LOVE *and the* BATTLEFRONT

Sabrina,
Thank you for the Support. Best Wishes,

LOVE
and the
BATTLEFRONT

ZACHARY H. WELSH

TATE PUBLISHING
AND ENTERPRISES, LLC

Love and the Battlefront

Published by Tate Publishing & Enterprises, LLC
127 E. Trade Center Terrace | Mustang, Oklahoma 73064 USA
1.888.361.9473 | www.tatepublishing.com

Tate Publishing is committed to excellence in the publishing industry. The company reflects the philosophy established by the founders, based on Psalm 68:11,
"The Lord gave the word and great was the company of those who published it."

Cover design by Jim Villaflores
Interior design by Jimmy Sevilleno

Published in the United States of America

ISBN: 978-1-62994-142-4
1. Fiction / War & Military
2. Fiction / Romance / General
14.01.17

DEDICATION

To the memory of all my fallen and wounded brothers and sisters—past, present, and future.

You are America's best.

God bless.

ACKNOWLEDGMENTS

I would like to acknowledge the Men who served with me; and that I had the privilege to sit down with and hear several of their stories. This story in fact is the story of many.

I would also like to thank my good friend and mentor, a man who helped me find the drive to seek publication and gave me guidance about not only publishing, but life. Dr. Michael Haynes. Thank you for the wisdom and friendship.

Finally I would like to thank my late grandmother Marjorie Thompson, who had a dream for one of her grandchildren to write a book or become an actor. The financial backing allowed me to get started, I am grateful. I am proud to have fulfilled one of those dreams.

CONTENTS

ABOUT THE AUTHOR

Zachary Welsh; is a United States Marine veteran. His experience in the corps has provided him with so many opportunities he may otherwise not have had, he has expressed his faith and praise in God who has blessed him in life. He was born in Houston, Texas, and spent his teenage years in a little po-dunk town called Rogers, Texas. As a Marine he enjoyed his time as a Machine Gunner in the infantry. He enlisted on June 26, 2005. The simple things in life are what he enjoys most, much due to the time he spent in Iraq. He believes that everyone needs to take the simple things serious and enjoy them, not take them for granted. He enjoys fishing and playing basketball. When he has time to spend with his family, he enjoys every moment of it.

PREFACE

The sound of gunshots and grenades played a very familiar tune in the background. The bullets whizzed by, whistling to the left and to the right, impacting all over the pothole-infested streets. Yet in the midst of the chaos and confusion, in the midst of the battlefield, Adam Green thought of her. She was his angel, a beautiful, young redhead named Leslie. He wanted more than anything to be with her and hoped that someday they would be together. *Snap, snap, snap.* Back to reality, as the rounds hit all around him. Once the realism of combat booted back up, he realized that not every day is guaranteed, and he began to write a letter to Leslie; he wanted her to know how he felt. The little voice inside kept saying, *Just tell her.* So he began to write.

Dear Leslie,

I really don't like doing this in a letter. There are just some things that I really want you to know, and I don't know if I'll get the chance to tell you…

EMOTIONS

NOVEMBER

THIS IS A simple story, a story about the struggles and the triumphs of life. There have been many gifts given from one to another, but the gift undisputedly above all is love.

"There is no greater love than that of someone that would lay down his own life for a friend." John 15:13 (NIV)

As we walked through the city in the armpit of the world—Mesopotamia, Iraq—you could see the death and destruction boiling up from underneath the earth. The smoke bellowed like that of a bonfire back home out in the middle of a cornfield. The terrain was sandy and rocky. There were a few million dollars in trash on the ground, just scattered randomly. If it had been recycled that's how much money it would be worth. The sky was baby blue with a few clouds dotted throughout one direction you looked, while toward the other was a wall of sand probably off about a hundred miles. That meant there would be another sandstorm that night. The air smelled of many different scents. There was the smell of trash, dirt, gasoline, feces, and the un-ignorable smell of blood. The smell of rotting corpses you can never get over. If you could ignore the others, blood was the one you could not.

The sound of gunshots and grenades played a very familiar tune in the background. The adrenaline muffles the sound though. We'd heard them like a clock ticking for the past two months, kind of got accustomed to it, or at least as accustomed to getting shot at as you could. The bullets were close yet they sounded like a black cat going off under water. Once we knew where they were coming from, they would stop and vanish, like a set of rims in Compton. We'd charge the house only to find empty ammunition brass casings. Run into the houses around it to find a family cowering below window level. "Where is he? Where is Ali Baba?"

"Mista, mista, no Ali Baba here." That was their answer for everything even if Ali Baba (the bad guy) was hiding in the other room. Then we'd go to the next house and the next. Ninety percent of the time we would come out empty handed, but every once in a while we would find an AK-47 or some grenades, and occasionally an insurgent.

The humvees were rolling around our position, bouncing up and down, trying to dodge the un-dodge-able potholes. The potholes didn't come from a lack of road maintenance, because we fixed the roads for them, but came from the constant IEDs (improvised explosive devices) and mortars. One side of the road would have rusty old oil drums on line. The other side had slabs of concrete missing from the road. They would drive the rough terrain throwing the poor gunner all around, circling the known enemy position. The driver would cut suddenly to avoid a pothole then jerk the wheel back to the other side.

Man, were we glad to have them there, mainly because either they would stop shooting at us and start on them, or they would run away altogether. The humvees would occasionally fire their heavy machine guns to suppress, to allow us to get closer to do our job and kick some doors in. Then they took a different road, whipping around the corner, throwing rocks and debris all over us just to get closer. That's when there was the huge flash of light and a cloud of dust, then the boom. There is no louder sound than that of the one that takes the lives of eighteen- to twenty-two-year-old heroes.

One of those heroes was a good buddy of mine; he was my roommate at one time. Like all of us, he knew what we signed up for. No, we didn't sign up to die for our country. We simply just wanted to make a difference in the world. When was the last time anything of national importance was solved without conflict from any party? Exactly! We remembered, unlike the people who protest us, saying they never did anything to us, "Send our boys home; they don't need to be over there." We remember, and we are not your boys. We are the "2,500-plus people lost on September 11th" boys. The ultimate price was just paid by the marines in that humvee in order to keep you arrogant, peace-loving, ignorant hippies and your kids in your peaceful home. That way you can sleep at night and not have to hear explosions off in the distance or even in your backyard.

The dust went high, and shrapnel from the up-armored ballistic humvee rained down on us along with oil, diesel, and hot, nearly melting asphalt. Fighting our way through the dust cloud, we ran over to the sight to find a crater the size of a full-size pool table and half a tire in the ground. We started calling their names in a confused blind hope. Maybe, just maybe we would find them alive. Then I hear, "I found Jamesport, I think."

"What do you mean 'you think'?"

We ran over there and found half of a boot; the other half was in the middle of someone else's spleen and intestines—that's where we found the dog tag. My heart immediately hit the floor. The day before Thanksgiving, all their parents, wives, girlfriends, brothers, and sisters would be finding out the bad news.

They had all died heroes, not from an enemy with any kind of balls; no, they were killed by the most cowardly enemy in the history of wars. They hide amongst the population, threaten, and take the lives of the families of those who may have the moral integrity to turn them in. They would hit you from a mile to two miles away with an improvised explosive device. They are smart, but they are the biggest cowards in the world. I snapped back into reality realizing the task at hand. I ran to gather my team and set up a perimeter around the position. Tactically, they would hit you, run off, then a few minutes later their buddies would come out with rocket-propelled grenades (RPG), and sure enough they did.

I heard my gunner say, "RPG, get down; everyone hit the deck!" The rocket whizzed right over us hitting a wall about twenty feet behind us. The QRF (quick reaction force) convoy rolled up as soon as the firefight started to perform the medevac. They started opening up with 7.62, 50-caliber machine guns and the Mark 19 automatic grenade launcher. We were all shooting everything we had; we had just lost good friends, we weren't gonna let this SOB get away.

The platoon commander began yelling, "Cease-fire!" So we passed it down the line to stop firing. The medevac chopper landed, and silently I said good-bye and a prayer for the families of the heroes. Everything was in slow motion; it seemed like anytime we saw that chopper, time started crawling. The images we saw flashed through our minds like a silent movie or a picture album. The walk back to the firm base was like walking the green mile. We were only about a mile from the base, but it just dragged on with regret. In the middle of the walk, I drifted off, back to my home.

I imagined my momma was there. She was wearing a blue nightgown, tucking in my little brother Trey, and he was crying. "I don't want Adam to die."

And she replied, "Don't worry, sweetie, your brother will be fine." I could tell in her tone that she was holding back the tears, trying to be strong for him. Hearing the strength and denial in her voice brought me to tears. I walked out and into the next room. My dad was there helping my other brother with his homework.

"The whole number and letter thing is confusing me, I can't help you here. Talk to Adam when he gets back."

My little brother Josh said in return, "Dad, when Adam gets home, I'll already have failed."

"Well, don't you have some girl you can call to do it for you?" Right there I just lost it. The thought of them growing up without a big brother to watch their football games or make fun of their girlfriends just broke me in two. A million miles away, and all I can do is fabricate scenes in my mind. I can't be there. And the possibility always lurks at the back of my mind that I may never be there again.

Next thing I know, we're getting shot at, just a quick little firefight. The gunman just shot a small burst, about ten rounds, then dropped his AK-47 and took off running into the palm groves along the Euphrates. The guy had almost done his homework. If someone shoots at us and drops their weapon, we're not supposed to shoot back. Notice how I said "not supposed to"; well, our 240 medium machine gun shot a five-round burst, four of which went from his groin to his head. The round that hit his head took from his left cheek to his left ear clean off. His body kept twitching as his brains drained out, and his body bled like syrup.

We all cheered seeing his lifeless body lying at the edge of the road. His white-and-black turban stained red with justice—three of our buddies taken from us—and finally we had a taste of revenge.

It crossed my mind that back in the states, most people, unless they had ever been in combat, would never fully understand the sacrifice we make on a daily basis. They won't understand our mindset—hell, they may even think we're crazy—but killing and surviving is our job. I'm not saying it's easy for us, 'cause it's not. You decide when a man dies; it's a trip. You wanna take it back, but you can't; then you think, *If I didn't get 'im, he might have got me, or worse, the buddy next to me.* There's not one day you don't think about what you would be doing if you didn't join—going to college, working for your dad, in jail, or starting a family, all of which would be better than seeing the stuff we've seen, the stuff we've done, which would be a permanent etch-a-sketch in our minds.

Now we were here at the bridge right out in front of the FOB (forward operating base). We would have to sprint across the bridge, my favorite part of the patrol. It was a one-hundred-meter sprint with about seventy pounds of gear and a seven- to eleven-pound weapon, after walking around for five hours not knowing if the next corner is your last. We made it though without a problem and walked up the hill to the base. We were walking around the corner to get debriefed from our platoon commander when it finally hit me, and I cried.

I cried like I had never cried before, and at the same time I prayed like I'd never prayed before.

The platoon commander began, "Marines, what you were a part of today will haunt you for the rest of your lives. No man should have to ever see what ya'll saw, but you saw it, and you were a part of it. You may ask yourselves, 'Why did this happen?' Gents, make no mistake. We are at war, and in war, unfortunately, people—no, heroes—lose their lives. You are in a fight for your lives. Your job is not to die for your country, it is to provide freedom for our country and the countries in ruins. You do this by arranging a meeting for the enemy with God. Lay waist to 'em. God can count the hair on your head; he can sort 'em out too. Cry, mourn for these men; do not hold your feelings inside. Tomorrow we will honor their memory and find the dogs that committed this atrocity and show them, or anyone thinking about doing what they did, what happens when marines get pissed off." He paused, reflecting before he continued emotionally. "Make sure the next opportunity you get to call your families, you do, and tell them you love them. Take the rest of the day to unwind and try to get some sleep. I know it will be tough, but try."

With that, most of us sat on our racks or our kevlars (helmet) thinking, crying, and a few would talk silently. You heard the whispers saying, "It was so sudden" or "Why them? They were good men." But mostly you heard revenge.

"Kill those dirtbags," or "They messed with the wrong marines."

The day went so slow you could see the dust settling or hear the creaks of the racks every time someone moved an inch. My ears were still ringing from the blast. I sat there and stared at the olive-drab sandbag windows. The sand leaked out of the sandbags like an hourglass. Trying to cry, wanting to cry, I was failing miserably. For some reason that still remains beyond me, I couldn't do it no matter how hard I tried. I found myself thinking of anything and everything sad; things that had happened or things that I'd done and now regret. Still, no matter what I thought of, I could not, I would not be able to cry, at least not right now.

This was not supposed to happen, never was this supposed to happen. We didn't want anyone to die; we knew it may happen, but not this violently.

Then the people had the nerve to play "the devil's prayer" over the mosque loud speaker. If the marines around hadn't already snapped, they just did. Since we'd been here, we started to associate the prayer with getting attacked. My buddy "T-rav" punched out part of the rock wall only to retract and find his knuckles bleeding. Most of us just cursed as loud as possible trying to drown out "Aaalllaaa aaakbaaaar," the only understandable thing in the whole prayer. The prayer played five times a day; once at 0430 then at 1145, and again at 1415, 1730, and 2100. You seemed to learn the times to the second after you heard it for three months straight. I pulled out my iPod and played some Rascal Flatts, "What Hurts the Most." I didn't really like it, but the song just seemed fitting for the time. As I began to listen and let the music take me away from this hell, a puppy poked its head around the corner.

My buddy Lee said with a smirk, "Think I can adopt him?"

I didn't think he could get a stray mutt to warm up to him, but sure enough he did. For a second, we were at peace, watching that little puppy, which we named Gizmo, prance around with no care in the world.

I tried to sleep that night but my mind ran rampant—thoughts of the family, of the marine, thoughts of my family. Sure enough, the sandstorm made it to us; it made the dark night even more opaque. The sweat from our body caught the sand and grime like a flytrap.

I thought of LCpl. Jamesport's mother and father receiving the news right before their Thanksgiving meal, the questions that they would ask, the answers they would get. They would not be told the whole story due to the graphic nature of it; they probably wouldn't even be told half of it. I imagined his mom screaming for justice, revenge, whatever she could get to avenge her baby's death; his father comforting his mother and eventually slipping back into the alcoholism he may have just overcome.

The thought of the man or men I/we had killed, and how we can do it so easily, because it is not an easy thing to do. There were thoughts of heaven and hell, life and death, right and wrong, moral and immoral. I thought of things I wish I would have done, things I wish I would have said, and I thought of her. I finally fell asleep after a long night of wrestling and burying my feelings and images I wished to forget.

I woke up that next morning at 0430 as the first prayer of the day played. I walked over three rooms down to where LCpl. Jamesport lived to check on him because it still hadn't hit me that he was gone, and he wasn't there. I was in denial, thinking everything from *maybe he's out on patrol right now* or *maybe he's at the shitters*. I just ignored the facts that all his gear was packed and ready to go home, and his section was all there sleeping; I just couldn't see the facts—I didn't want to see the facts. I needed to, but I didn't want to. His bunkmate looked up at me with extremely heavy eyes and said, "Dude, he's really gone. This shit's no joke; they're out there to kill us." I just looked at him and sighed and shook my head, then turned and walked out.

The time now was about 0800, probably a little bit later; I'm not exactly sure. I was down in the chow hall with a couple of the guys from my squad eating muffins, the blueberry ones. Muffins and beef jerky can get people through just about anything. They are definitely favored by the armed forces around the world. Then the mortars started hitting. The first one hit and sounded more like a grenade than a mortar; that's how far off they were. It probably ended up hitting a house in the middle of the city. One of the posts that could see the impact called over the radio that we were having a mortar attack. Another one hit a few minutes later, then another. Every time one hit, the sound and the rumble in the ground got louder, more powerful, and closer; almost like a boxer's fist, slowly but steadily working away at the body just waiting for the power swing, then going in for the kill. They were walking them on target, us being the target. We all reached for our gear and threw it on, in what had to be only two seconds. I guess it's sort of being blind to the truth, because if a mortar landed in the room we were in, we would have all been dead, with or without gear. The fourth impact hit when I drifted off in my own world again.

I was walking through the school hallway; it was my first day of my junior year. I found where my locker was and all my classes. I then walked around to find all my buddies when I ran into one girl who always had a crush on me. We talked for a few minutes about how each other's summers were.

Then she said, "Oh, and in case you were wondering, I got a boyfriend now." She said it in that trying-to-make-you-jealous kind of voice with a smirk.

I just looked at her, smiled, and said, "Well, congratulations. I hope he's a great guy."

Shortly after that little conversation is when she walked through the door. It was the first time I'd ever seen her—an angel. Time slowed down for a minute. Her bouncy red hair teased the eyes as it brushed her shoulders. Her eyes were hazel, on the green side, and her skin was fair, soft as silk. Her body was perfectly shaped, heavenly. The students moved out of her way, parting the hallway like the Red Sea. She walked so smooth; it almost looked as if she were gliding across the floor. She played softball, so she had firm, muscular legs. I, for the first time in my life, knew exactly what I wanted, and it was her. However, she was already with someone; a short, stubby, shaggy-haired kid. To say the least, he was a slightly less-than-attractive boy. He treated her as if she were less than a dog, which she didn't deserve; no girl deserved that. But like so many confused young women, she always went back. I wanted to be a hero, swoop in and save the day, but I couldn't grow the balls to talk to her. She was just too beautiful and too perfect. I was speechless. Her name was Leslie. I hoped that someday I would just maybe have a chance. First though, I'd have to make it out of this hellhole.

Now I had had this dream before several times since I joined the Marine corps. It was more or less a missed memory. I spoke to her occasionally at church; to be honest, she was the only reason I went. Her family had sent me a few packages with socks and cookies, so I figured I would write her a letter of thanks and appreciation. Depending on how she responded to that, or if she responded to it, I might write her one on how I felt about her. I thought of her a lot; thought what I would have said, what I would have done, if I could do it all again. Then, just as quickly as the lights had gone out in my head, they came back on. It was reality once again.

All together, they launched six mortars at us, gradually walking them on to our base. Suddenly they stopped.

Just as fast as it had started, it was over. The all-clear sound came about thirty minutes after the last one hit. We picked up our plates of chow and continued eating as if nothing had happened. "That's a lot of collateral damage; those bastards couldn't hit us if we stood on top of their mortar tubes," one of my buddies joked. Me, I just prayed a prayer of thanks for the protection that had just been afforded to us.

I went back to my berthing space to try and get some sleep before I had to go out on patrol. We were scheduled to be out for twelve hours in an anti-sniper position. Basically, to be politically incorrect, we were gonna be enemy sniper bait for twelve hours. The chain of command made many bright decisions during our tour, mainly at the company level. Our job was to go set up in a series of houses and walk back and forth through the windows so that they would shoot at us, and our snipers could find their position. I had lain down in my rack just long enough to get told to take the trash up to the burn pit. We burned our trash along with our feces in order to keep the base as sanitary as possible, seeing as we didn't have any plumbing or garbage men to pick our trash up. It was a third-world country littered with disease, diseases even the most intellectual of doctors hadn't heard of.

Meanwhile, inside the command post, all the higher ups were talking about combat replacements for the mounted section that had lost the marines. My name was given up because I was a machine gunner, and I would best be able to replace the previous turret gunner. Being mounted was the last thing I wanted, because two-thirds of the deaths in Iraq were from IEDs, which the primary target of are humvees.

The hour to push out on our suicide mission was approaching rapidly. We prepared our gear, grabbed some MREs (meals ready to eat), and cleaned our rifles as the deadline approached. I ran over immediate action drills in my head on what to do if something happened. Truth be told though, rehearsing and reviewing only go so far, then comes heart. Heart is what gets people through tough situations and surreal events. No amount of practice can prepare you for the realism of combat. We piled it in for the brief, though we already knew exactly what our mission was. After the brief, I grabbed a cup of coffee quickly before we stepped off, said a prayer, and read my laminated Psalm 23:4.

> Yea though I walk through the valley
> Of the shadow of death
> I will fear no evil
> For thou art with me
> Thy rod and thy staff
> They comfort me

I had the verse memorized; hell, I had it tattooed on my ribcage, but reading the words always seemed to comfort me, so I read it a lot. We went into silent mode and stepped off. We were always silent to hide our movement, even though most of the time they knew exactly where we were. We were fighting in their country, the place where they'd grown up; of course they knew where we were.

We walked down the hill, away from our base, headed toward one of the schools off of a no-named road. This was the road we called grenade ally simply because if you walk down it or drove down it, you are more likely to get a grenade thrown at you than not. When we turned the corner right by the school, our point man said, "The kids are at recess; keep an eye out for grenades." As sad as that sounds, the kids were normally the ones to throw grenades at us. There were thirteen of us in the patrol. We were about halfway past the school when a barrage of rocks came over the wall. We took cover and threw stun grenades back. We almost threw real grenades until someone yelled, "They're just rocks, stun um!"

They got lucky. We should have charged the school, and according to the laws of war, it would have been completely right in doing so; but our mission stated that we must get to our objective as soon as possible and only stop in emergency situations. So as soon as we had the situation under control, we got the signal to double time (run). We were about a mile and a half from the block we were supposed to be in, but adrenaline and heart kicked in; we lugged our gear, and our dirty, tired, worn bodies at a little bit slower than a dead sprint pace until we got there. Man, I hated running.

When we arrived, we charged through the door and cleared the house. There was no one there. We ran to the second deck and cleared it too; no one. It was when the house was empty that we were in the most danger, because the insurgents didn't have to worry about collateral damage.

For some reason, I wasn't scared though, and not being scared terrified me. Then we took turns walking back and forth through the window. Each person would walk back and forth for thirty minutes while the others rested and ate. We all took turns pacing through the danger space for twelve hours. Nothing happened. The still of night had fallen upon us like a silently stalking shadow.

While I had been on my rest period, some of my buddies played poker. They had a brand new deck of Bicycles that had come in a USO care package. When I was invited to join in, I declined; my mind was elsewhere. I was…the only real way to describe it would be miserably happy thinking of Leslie. I wrote nine different letters to Leslie explaining how I felt about her, none of which I deemed good enough to send, none of which were ever the same. I kept a few of them, but the majority I crumbled up and set on fire. As I watched the ashes float away into the ever-cooling evening breeze, I thought of the last time I had been home and what I wish I would have done. I traveled back in thoughts to an earlier memory before I was over here in this mess.

I got home on pre-deployment leave, around the time she was starting her senior year in high school. I was determined that I would talk to her more than the occasional hello and small talk. So I went to church to see her. My heart fluttering from nervousness, I had the whole conversation planned out, and still somehow

I didn't have the words to say. It was like the first time I saw her on that magical day she walked through the hallway, time slowed down. Her hair hadn't changed much, it was just slightly shorter. She had gained some weight though, but nonetheless she was still amazingly beautiful. I couldn't take my eyes off of her as she walked down the aisle. I hoped that she couldn't feel me gazing at her. Then she made eye contact, and I held it for a second then looked away. I looked back; she looked back at me and ducked her head in what looked like shame. It was confusing. I turned to my mom and asked, "What's the deal with Leslie?"

She replied, "Oh, it's been rumored around town that she's pregnant. She's probably a little self-conscious."

"Well, Mom, you know how I feel about her. When were you gonna tell me?"

She said, "I thought you already knew, and besides, I don't want to take part in spreading rumors. You know how this town works. I'm gonna ask her after the service today. I'll let you know. Why don't you just talk to her, Adam, let her know how you feel?"

I smiled nervously. "Momma, your boy's a marine, but that doesn't mean I'm not scared to talk to an angel."

That made her chuckle just a little bit. She just said, "I love you, son, but in order for you two to ever get together, you're gonna have to talk to her."

"Well, here goes nothing."

I talked to myself about what to say and told myself there was nothing to be nervous about. Then I was there, standing right next to her. She looked at me. I looked away in a hurry. I was terrified. As I started to walk off, she said energetically, "Well...am I gonna get a hug? I haven't seen you in a while."

I turned back to face her and muttered, "Hey, Leslie, how have you been?" Then I bent down and gave her a hug, a hug I would cherish through Iraq.

She said, "I've been good. Your mom was telling me you're getting ready to go to Iraq."

Out of nowhere, I gained the slightest bit of confidence and said, "Yea, the end of this month. Say you wanna hang out sometime, you know, to catch up?" Immediately my heart hit the ceiling. I had done it—I had finally asked.

She softly replied, "I would love to, but I work every day except Sunday. I'll give you my number, though, so you can call me some time...And you better call me!"

I was in a roller coaster of emotions and just said, "Sounds good." She laughed a happy laugh. It was right then and there I knew I would someday fall in love with this beautiful girl. I may have even fallen in love with her right there. It's kind of funny how love can be the best but most confusing thing on earth. I got her number and began walking back to my pew. I called only once.

Meanwhile, my mom and dad were talking. My mom said, "You just watch, Adam is gonna wanna marry that girl."

My dad looked at Leslie, then me, then my mom and said in a sarcastic manner, "I'm sure he does."

I didn't know what my parents were talking about, and as soon as I sat down, I said, "I'm gonna marry that girl someday."

Momma just looked at my dad and smiled then said, "How well do I know my son?"

❧

Then the call came over the radio, about thirty minutes after the sunset, to get back to the base and to do it in a most discreet manner, which meant we were running the whole way back.

When we arrived at the FOB, we received our debrief. Then they told us we had a follow-on mission at 0100. We were to raid a group of houses right outside the base. They had received some intel (intelligence) that there was a meeting of HVIs (high-value individuals) and this was the only time we would be able to snag them.

❧

After the brief, our SSgt (staff sergeant) said, "Hey, Green, I need to see you."

"Yes, staff sergeant." That's when he hit me with the news.

He said, "Hey, you're not goin' out with us tonight. The MAP section (mounted assault platoon) needs casualty replacements, and you're one of the best machine gunners we got, so you're gonna be in the turret on the MK19." I knew my place, and he outranked me.

I did not want to be mounted but I had no choice, so I just said, "Aye, aye, staff sergeant."

I turned to leave. He stopped me and said, "Hey, Green, you're a good kid. Keep your eyes open, and bring um hell."

I turned my head, nodded, and said, "Good to go, staff sergeant. Take care."

I went back to my room and told my boys good-bye then silently packed my gear and cleaned my weapon. When I was done packing, I grabbed all my things and lugged them over to the MAP sections berthing area, rolled my sleeping bag on the ground, and kicked my boots off to use them as a pillow. I scrolled through my iPod, didn't find anything appealing, so I put it on random. The song that played was "When I'm Gone" by Three Doors Down. I'd had a long, exhausting day full of emotion and wandering thoughts. I said the same prayer I said every night. I asked God for protection and thanked him for the protection he'd provided me. I asked him to keep my family safe at home. I asked him to give Leslie a man who could love and take care of her and be a good father to her beautiful newborn baby boy named Tyson, and to give him a good father who could love and care for him as his own. Then last, I prayed for God to give me a woman whom I can love and care for and settle down with. I never once asked for her because I wanted her to be happy, and I may not be that man for her. I said amen, then I slept, like I hadn't slept since I'd joined the corps, like a baby.

LETTERS AND GLORY

DECEMBER 24

IT WAS THE day before Christmas. I had been mounted for about a month now; the initial nervousness had worn off. When I first got thrown into it, however, I was terrified. My convoy of three humvees and a seven-ton truck hadn't been hit since the last incident that landed me here. We as a whole had found eleven IEDs, which was amazing because of the concealment. They would pour diesel on the asphalt and burn it in order to loosen up the ground then dig a hole to bury the IED in the middle of the road. Next, they would fill it in and re-tar it in a matter of hours, making it next to invisible to the naked eye.

My eyes were heavy from the lack of sleep. We had been in a blocking position along the Euphrates River hidden in the palm groves for two days now. The palm trees were in rows like corn and were taller than any palm trees I'd ever seen. The they were very luscious and green because of the natural irrigation from the river. The river itself flowed with a strong visible current, running around the few islands in the middle. Boat traffic was no longer allowed because we had been shot at several times from the fleeing boats. The road we were on was one of the better ones in the area. I could only see three potholes from my nest.

There were three people in my truck, so we took turns on fire watch, two-hour shifts. It was about time for the sun to start peaking over the river. If I wasn't in Iraq it would have, and in some way it was kind of peaceful. It was more or less not as much paranoia than peace. I had about an hour left on my watch before I could try to catch some sleep which most likely wouldn't happen. The sky was full of stars starting to fade into the day. When the sun finally broke the night to day, it was majestic. The sky was full of morning colors. The clouds were stained with pinks and blues and a miraculous white; they were huge and fluffy. The sky reflected off the rippling current of the smooth flowing Euphrates. As I sat there absorbing the fresh morning air, I thought to myself, *I have never stayed up just to watch the sun come up*, and I thought, *I'll do this when I get back home.* I started to appreciate the beauty of nature; every little thing had its own little light it gave to the world. When I thought of the beauty in that simple sunrise, I saw Leslie. Now though, the lack of sleep started to catch up with me. My head bobbed once, so I reached inside my pack and pulled out my notebook. I was thinking about Leslie, as I always did, and I knew that writing my feelings down would help me stay awake for that last hour.

Thoughts of my past caught up with me once again. The music played loud, but not quite loud enough to where you couldn't hear the person across the table. It was prom, my senior year, and I had taken my girlfriend at the time. She was a very pretty petite little blonde girl named Tori. We were sitting there talking. She kept trying to get me to dance; I would tell her I don't know how.

And she would say with a happy-go-lucky smile, "Come on, I'll teach ya!" I really wasn't that great of a dancer, but I could hold my own. I had only planned on dancing with her once that night; I had really just gone for the environment and to hang out with my buddies. You could feel the young high school hearts beating with passion, nervousness, and premature love.

Now I liked Tori a lot, but even then when Leslie walked through the door, I felt my heart skip a beat. She and her boyfriend broke up at the time. They would date long enough to piss each other off and then break it off; they had that kind of relationship. They went together anyhow and just parted ways once they got in the door. I really hated seeing them together because I knew, or had at least heard of how he treated her, and it was wrong. I found myself staring at her. When she made eye contact with me, immediately I looked away. She had her hair up in a bun with the excess length flowing out of it. Her face had been painted on. She had that kind of natural beauty; I didn't imagine her having to use that much make-up. Her lips shined from the gloss, and her face sparkled from the ever-so-slight glitter. Her dress was silver, and it fit her figure perfectly. It was low in the back, just above the tail bone. In the front, there was a low-cut flowery lace design just high enough to still be modest. I guess the best way to describe her would be beautiful. I was afraid my girlfriend had seen me staring, so I decided right there to ask her to dance in order to lower the suspicion. I would also feel less guilty about asking Leslie to dance later if I had already danced with Tori a few times.

My heart was fluttering as I walked over to Leslie; I was going to ask her to dance. I knew she would say yes, but that didn't ease my nervousness any. I got up to her and tapped her on the shoulder lightly. As I admired her beautiful eyes, I asked, "Leslie, you wanna dance next song?"

She smiled at me and giggled, which got my heart racing for fear of rejection, then said, "Sure, I'd love to."

The next song began to play. I grabbed her hand then warned her. "Hey, I'm not that great of a dancer; you'll have to forgive me." As we glided around the floor, I soaked in the evening like a sponge and made small talk. I'm sure the dance meant nothing to her, but it meant the world to me—spinning around the floor holding her hand and the small of her back.

Then the music ended. With a simple thanks, she daintily walked back to her table as I walked back to mine. My soul ached knowing that may very well be the last time I ever danced with an angel, maybe the last time I held the most beautiful woman on earth. Again, reality crept back in.

"MAP 5-1, MAP 5-1, return to base."

It was about time. I ducked down from my turret and woke my driver and VC (vehicle commander) up, telling them the news. I had begun to think they were gonna leave us out there until Christmas Day. We started rolling back to the FOB around 0800, set to arrive 0830. As we pulled out of our blocking position, we followed in the tracks of the vehicle in front of us. The seven-ton truck turned the corner to drive across the bridge.

We were only about 1800 meters from where we had come from when there was a huge explosion. At first it was so loud and powerful I thought we were hit. My ears immediately started ringing; the flash that I had seen last time was right on our truck. I checked to see if my legs were still there, they were. Then I realized we weren't the ones hit. I turned around only to get hit by part of a front axle in the face. It stung for a split second before the adrenaline kicked in. I saw the huge cloud of dust, and the whole front half of the truck disintegrated.

The first thing out of my mouth was "Casualties! Call in a medevac!" Though I screamed at the top of my lungs, I couldn't hear the words coming out of my mouth and yelled again. I'd been here before, and the memory I did not wish to repeat.

Then a miracle happened. Their driver crawled out of the truck, turned to grab his weapon, and said, "Ha, ha, punks you didn't get us!"

I yelled at him, "Is everyone alright?"

He just looked at me, smiles and says, "Yea, they're good too."

Not even a minute after they had all crawled out of the truck, we started taking small arms fire from a row of buildings off to the left. Our staff sergeant yelled above the chaos, "Get those guns up!" I didn't have to be told twice. Without any hesitation, I racked my charging handles. Condition 2. I racked it back again, hearing the zing of the bullets flying over the turret. I stood up, aimed in, and launched three grenades. I was off by about five meters to the left, and with a quick swing of the turret, I shot another three dead on.

The gunner in the truck next to us on the .50 cal screams, "Green, where are they? I can't see them!"

I launch another three. As they exploded, I yelled back, "Right there!" My machine gunner instinct kicked in, and I yell at him again, "Talking guns. I fire *boom, boom, boom*; you fire *da da da da,* traverse across the building, *boom, boom, boom.* I shoot windows, you *da, da, da, da* tear the building apart." He nodded his head as a bullet hit my turret and ricocheted, smacking into my kevlar (helmet).

We laid waste to the building for about thirty seconds more when I hear DB the other gunner say, "Shit, I think I'm hit!"

I yelled at my driver to get me more ammo as I shot off my last few bursts. My head ached, maybe from the explosion, or the ricochet, or maybe all the rounds I fired, but now wasn't the time to think about anything but getting out of here alive. When I ran out of ammo, I grabbed my M16 and started shooting it as fast as my finger could pull the trigger. Two magazines go by before I get my machine gun ammo. I load a belt of twelve. I was fed up with getting shot at, so I aimed for the far left corner of the building and pressed the trigger, working my way to the right side all twelve rounds. The front of the building collapsed, and the marines in the truck who had been blown up, meanwhile, had been moving into a position to flank the building. As soon as it fell, they ran up, with grenades ready, to the side windows and threw four grenades into the window. As soon as the last grenade blew, they jumped thru the window to clear the building. "All clear, enemy neutralized," I heard over the squad radio.

They came back over the hook a few minutes later, saying, "Great shootin'. We got ten inside and four scattered throughout the backyard."

Now that we were fairly safe, I had time to duck inside the truck and take my helmet off. I poured some water on my head to cool it down. "Hey there, Green, that's the shit I'm talkin' about. Hell yea, you definitely got some," my VC said. I just look at him with heavy eyes and dirty, oily water dripping off my face and nodded. I had a small cut on the side of my neck, didn't know what from, still don't.

I got out to inspect my work, thinking I would be happy. As I walked in, the stench of gunpowder and death hit my nose. I kept walking, then the smell moved to my stomach, and I couldn't hold back the vomit but kept walking. The throw-up flowing from my mouth to the blood-soaked floor bounced on my boots. The images since then I have tried to erase from my mind with no avail. I don't like to talk about what I saw that day, so I won't. I felt horrible for some reason. Why? They blew us up then tried to shoot us up. Still, thoughts of morality, right and wrong teased me like a fly on raw meat. *What would people back home think about the things we did, the things we saw?*

The QRF unit rolled up on scene with litters ready to medevac wounded, but there were none, only us and a lot of dead. They took all the enemy weapons and paraphernalia, and we left as a huge eight-vehicle convoy as a wrecker convoy towed the blown-up vehicle away.

We finally pulled back in to the FOB at 1030. There were chicken wings for lunch, which were a rare delicacy but always a treat. I got about halfway done eating my plate when my staff sergeant walked in and said, "Green, the CO (company commander) wants to talk to you." I gave the rest of my wings away and reported in.

"Good morning, Sir, Lance Corporal Green reporting as ordered."

He smiled and said, "At ease, take a seat." I sat down knowing full well what I was in there for. I was nervous, because if I had broken any law of war, I could get fried.

Instead, however, he said, "Hey, we're proud of you. SSgt. Kay has recommended you for the NAM (Navy and Marine Corps Achievement Medal) for your quick reaction to the ambush and how well you handled yourself out there. From my understanding, you were directing two trucks also."

"Well, sir, I was trained well and just did my job."

He replied, "From the looks of it, son, you may get a Purple Heart too. You got a little scratch on your face and neck. I think you deserve that, but I don't think you deserve the NAM for reasons you explained. The marine corps doesn't hand out medals for just doing your job. However, I will get you a CIRCOM (certificate of accommodation) because you did do your job in an exemplary manner."

"Thank you, sir, but I don't want a Purple Heart for some scratches. I have buddies who are missing limbs, and I think getting one for a scratch would be demeaning to their sacrifice."

"Well, the marine corps says that any wound suffered during combat operations deserves a Purple Heart. So I'm still gonna recommend you for that."

"Sir, I appreciate it, but please don't. I will be offended and won't wear it."

He looked at me like I was crazy, smiled, and said, "Very well, carry on with your day. And Green...keep up the good work."

"Aye, aye, sir. Good morning, sir." I stood up and walked out.

I went to my room, trying to hide out. I didn't want to talk to anyone right now; I just wanted to be alone for a minute to gather my thoughts. People, however, kept walking in, wanting to hear my story. I'd tell um, "Talk to my driver, he saw it."

They'd go to him, and he'd say, "Talk to Green; he can explain it better than I can." Then I'd end up having to tell them. They would look with intent eyes, wanting to hear every little detail.

They'd say, "Man, you should get like a Bronze Star or NAM or something."

I would just nod and say, "I guess."

I never spoke of the awards I turned down. I didn't think I was worthy. Even if I was, I wasn't a ribbon chaser and didn't really care. I never tried to be a hero; I just tried to get back home. Leslie was my angel, and I wanted to see her.

When story time finally ended, I crawled in my rack, threw my poncho over my head and cried. I was emotionally and physically drained, tired from three days of nothingness. I thought about how I felt about Leslie and how she would never know. I thought about missing my little brother's entire football season and how I wished I could have been there to watch them, or been there with Leslie when she had her beautiful son on the 16th of November. I realized that not every day is guaranteed and that I might not make it out, so I began to write a letter to Leslie. I wanted her to know how I felt. The little voice inside kept saying *just tell her*. So I began to write.

Dear Leslie

I really don't like doing this in a letter. There are just some things that I really want you to know, and I don't know if I'll get to tell you.

Please read the whole thing. When I joined the marine corps, I was happy. I had done something not many people do, then I was gone so long without being there to see Josh and Trey grow up. I started to see things in my life I wished I would have done or would have said, but I couldn't do them or say them. It really broke my heart to see my brothers grow up in some of the most important years of their lives without me. I believe that everyone has someone that they have a deep caring for and affection for. For me, that person is you, Leslie. I'm not asking you to be that for me, I'm just asking for the opportunity to show you who I am. As much as I regret what I did, or did not do, for, with, or say to my family, I regret not talking to you more, getting to know you better, hanging out with you. I'm not saying that you would have opened up to me or hung out with me, but I could have at least tried more. I wish I would have. I was always scared, still am, I'm scared to death, really. But I'd rather tell you what I'm thinking instead of living with a what-if conscience every day. I know I'm not the best letter writer ever; you'll have to forgive me I'm givin' it a shot though. I don't mind getting emotional; however, I do mind doing it in a letter, but from my standpoint I don't know if I'll get the chance to tell you face to face.

When I first saw you in the hallway my junior year, you were a freshman, I thought you were the prettiest girl I had ever seen. I still do. But I saw you with Robby, and I admit I was jealous, I still am jealous. Then I started talking to you, getting to know you a little bit, and I saw who you really are. You are not only a beautiful young lady, you were always happy or at least put on a good show, you were nice to everyone, you talked to me, lol. You're smart, athletic. You could probably kick my butt at softball... if I let you, j/k. Then you started coming to my church. You know I'm not the churchiest guy around. I used to hate going, I'd tell my parents I had to work just to not have to go, then go ride around Temple. That's a secret, they still don't know that, shhh. But anyway, when you started going, I wanted to go just to sit in the back and talk to you all service. I was jealous of Zack and Matt, you being good friends with them, and me and you just talking occasionally. At my senior prom, I wanted to take you and was going to ask you, but you had already been asked by, forgive me if I'm wrong, Jason. But you and Robby went instead. So I took Tori, because Keith told me she really wanted to go, and we started dating after I found out you and Robby got back together, so I took her. Then when I got to dance with you, that made my night. I know I wasn't that great. I think I stepped on you a time or two.

Your mom and my mom started to be friends, and then my momma adopted you, lol. Well, about the time that happened, I went to boot camp. To be honest, it wasn't that hard physically, but it was very lonely you were trapped inside hell for three months without any communication. Then I came home on leave for ten days and saw you at church a time or two but couldn't bring myself to talk to you. Then I came home around Christmas, and the same thing, I couldn't do it. I got stationed in Hawaii, which by the way is beautiful, but the whole time I was in paradise I thought of you.

I found out you were pregnant in early August, kind of out of the loop, huh. I was happy for you; really I was and still am happy for you. I can imagine how tough it has been, and is, and will be, but you can do it, I know you can. Besides, when you had Tyson, you accomplished in one day what many mothers spend their lives trying to do. You became the hottest mom in the world! Congratulations! Tyson has a great mom and I'm sure you will raise him to be a great young man. When I found out you were pregnant, I realized I may be too late and that's why I'm writing this. Leslie, I just want a chance to show you who I am, and who I can be for you and Tyson. I'm not asking anything of you because I know it's gonna be tough for you to jump in a relationship. I'm just saying I want to get to know you and be there for you if you want me to. If not, I understand I probably blew my chance a long time ago. If not, please don't hate me or think less of me for this. Please just know the whole thing is the truth. Please write me back and just let me know what you think or how you feel. With that said, I close this letter. Thanks for reading, take care, and don't give up hope.

Sincerely,
Adam

I revised, reread, and reviewed the letter a million times it seemed before it was good enough; I never thought it was though. I went to my buddy Mike and showed him the product. He looked at me and said, "You really like this one, don't you?" I nodded and he continued saying, "Well, this can go one of two ways; either she'll think you're sweet and give you the time of day, or she'll think you're weird and need to stop stalking her. I know you're not a stalker, but she doesn't. It's up to you, man."

I said, "I really need her to know how I feel, I'll take my chances...Man, I can't send it, I don't know what it is; I'm just scared of what she'll say."

He smiled and said, "Well, do you want her to know what you think about her or not? You'll never get her attention if you don't."

I shrugged with a nervous smile. "Yea, I want her to know." Before I could finish my sentence, he had taken the letter and put it in an envelope.

He said, "I know you, Green. You'll go back to your room and rip it up, just like you have the last five. I'm sending it out for you." I was glad for this, because he was right. If he didn't do it, it would never get done.

Seven hours till midnight and tomorrow would be Christmas. Hopefully I would get some rest. It had been a long time since I had got a full night's sleep. To tell you the truth, I don't think that even if I had the time to, I could. I lay down, stared at the top bunk, listened to some music, and prayed, thanking God for protection and for the life that I had led.

We went out two more times that day, finally getting done for the day at 0100. I slept and woke up on and off all night until 0600. Merry Christmas.

CHRISTMAS

THE CLUB

It was Christmas afternoon, and our job was to escort people to and from our FOB for Christmas chow, which consisted of turkey and dressing, stuffing and yams. There was pecan and apple pies for dessert. The goal of our mission was to get everyone back; that way they could enjoy the meal and attempt to call their families. We shuttled people back and forth from 0900 to1500, with a thirty-minute-long chow break in the middle. I think we had the best cooks in our battalion; they seemed to be able to make a nice decent-tasting meal, whatever it may be, out of nothing. It was either that, or I was so hungry all the time that anything tasted good.

I called home for the first time since I'd been here. I'd had the opportunity to call a few times but knew the sound of their voices would break me in two. To tell you the truth, I only called because I knew it would mean the world to them. I was calling them at around 1700, which meant it would be about 7:00 a.m. there, just turning Christmas Day.

I imagined what they would be doing. Dad would have beaten the sun up, as he so often does. He'd be sitting out on the dock that hovered over our pond waiting for the sun to rise. Maybe that, or he'd be in the living room reading a few chapters from the Bible. Mom would wake up and cook what she called Christmas eggs. They had American cheese and green olives with the pimientos still in them. My mouth watered just thinking about them. My little brothers would be waking up to the smell. Then they'd eat as a family; say a prayer of thanks and for me. After breakfast, one of my little brothers would say, "Can we open presents now?"

My mom would jokingly return with, "Ya'll got coals this year." They would then sit around our adopted little Charlie Brown tree. We always got the smallest, most pathetic tree we could find every year then see if we could get it to grow. It never worked. They would spend the rest of the day playing with whatever they got, or float on the pond fishing all afternoon. Then they'd go to bed and sleep without fear.

So I called; I'd had enough of these illusory memories. It rang three times before my mom answered the phone. In a tired, groggy voice, she said, "Hello, may I ask whose calling?"

"Sure you can ask; it's someone who loves you very much."

I could hear a huge smile in her voice as she yelled across the house. "'Gary, pick up the phone! Adam's calling.' Adam how are you doing? It's so good to hear your voice?"

I smiled, holding back the tears and trying to sound strong. "I'm good, and it's great to hear your voice too. Merry Christmas, how's everyone doing?"

"We're good, Dad just picked up."

He said, "Hey, boy, how they treatin' you?"

"Well, minus being in Iraq...they treat me good." I was at a loss for words. There was so much I wanted to say but didn't know just quite how to say it. So instead, I just said, "Sorry, I haven't called." I was more or less trying to comfort myself than them.

Momma just replied, "It's okay, sweetie. You calling is the best present I could ask for, and besides, we know you're busy and probably don't have much time." This was true; I didn't have all the time in the world. I had imagined the conversation going something like this. However, when she asked, "How are you doing emotionally? Has anything bad happened?" I had to lie. I couldn't leave them with the thought of me being in danger, so I bit my tongue and said, "I'm good. It's not that bad out here. You have nothing to worry about, but keep praying for me." I knew they knew I was lying. I could hear it in their voices, so instead, we made small talk about Josh and Trey and how they did during their football seasons, or how they were doing in school. I asked about Leslie and told my mom to tell her hi for me. My time was up. We were only allotted fifteen minutes on the phone because everyone was trying to call home today. "Well, I love ya'll both, tell Josh and Trey the same."

"We love you too and so do your brothers, stay safe, and always you will be in our prayers." I wanted to be at home so bad right now I could feel it in my body.

I fought the tears and said, "I love you too, buh-bye." It hurt to hear their voices, but then again I knew it would. Anytime I got a letter or wrote one, I could feel the words like a needle straight through the heart. I wanted to be home, I wanted to go fishing with my brothers or try to talk to Leslie. I found it most difficult in the spare time I had to not think about her. I wondered what she would think about my letter, or if she would even think about it. Would she write me back?

The day was about gone; it had been a peaceful Christmas considering the situations. As I walked back to my room, I heard music bumping down the hall and the conversations of the guys hanging outside the room. I walked through all the smokers relaxing in the doorway and opened my door to find...a club scene. The lights were off, with two guys on opposite sides of the room moving their surefire flashlights like strobe lights and another marine on the top of one of the bunks waving around a red lens flashlight. There was tassel hanging from the ceiling and about fifteen guys havin' a great time. Everyone was dancing, forgetting about all the bad things.

One of my roommates yelled above the music, "Welcome to club 5-1, we poppin' all night tonight, we'll be open every night we're back at 1800."

Now I have a major problem with dancing, I look like a fish out of water, but that didn't stop me from loosening up and enjoying myself. For a little while, all my worries drifted away like a raging river lost in the sound. I just thought about having a good time, and I did. The cha-cha was the next song on DJ Danbizzle's list. Everyone slid and stomped, and we did our best to go down low all the way to the flo'. It was a great night, one of the better I had, Christmas night at club 5-1 Iraq.

We opened the club up as often as possible, attracting new clubbers or spectators every time. People would walk in and laugh or bring their video cameras to show friends back home what a bunch of marines do when they're bored. It wasn't necessarily that we were bored as it was that we needed something to relieve some stress. The club was our outlet—our saving grace—it allowed us to keep our sanity.

When the club closed, I went to the chow hall to get a muffin and a cup of coffee. For some reason, coffee in the evening puts me to sleep, and it did just that. I had to get up early the next morning to make a supply run. So I was great full for the sleep that I so easily slid into.

"Stop, stop, stop!" I woke up screaming in a cold sweat. It was the middle of the night. I had about two hours before I'd have to wake up. I was terrified, I never dreamed really; and most of the time I did, they weren't good. I had seen an IED and was trying to warn my driver. He just couldn't hear me. As soon as it blew on us, I had awakened. Now I just lay there, unable to fall back to sleep. Leslie was on my mind now, taking a little bit of the stress away. I could probably go back to sleep, but honestly I would rather sit there and think of her and how, if I ever got with her, I would do my best to make her happy. I thought and thought some more, then I got woken up again. It was time to go do our supply run. I got ready, shaved, brushed my teeth, then went to my buddy Mike's room and chatted for a while about what we were gonna get when we got back. I got some coffee, ate a Snickers I'd got in a package, then threw my gear on and went out to the trucks. I sat there in full gear enjoying the morning breeze.

PAIN

JANUARY–FEBRUARY

"HEY, GET EVERYONE outside for pictures. Full gear. We have to have them turned in by tomorrow for the float book."

"Roger that, staff sergeant." I said. A float book is like a high school yearbook. I ran around for the next ten minutes getting all our guys from the room or chow hall. I had to run to the head to find the last two guys. They ran out with half shaves and toothpaste still waiting on the brushes. When we all got out there, staff sergeant got our picture then prepared us for a brief.

It was the same brief we had heard for the past five months—we were going on a re-supply run up to headquarters battalion. The route was the same, everything was the same, but I had a bad feeling about today. I had felt this way several times before, so I just brushed it under the rug. We had all been up for three days now, out on constant detaining missions and just your regular patrol. Going to the re-supply point just meant that we would have enough downtime when we got there to make us even more tired than we already were. The morning was a little bit overcast but still kind of nice in its own way.

I ran over to Mike's room, woke him up, and told him, "We're gonna get a coffeepot when we get back, write that on the list."

He nodded and said, "So why did you wake me up?"

"Well, don't you want a cup of coffee now?"

With a groggy smile, he said, "You're right. Were gettin' a coffeepot, now get the hell outta here, I'm tired."

"Later, bro," I said then ran back to my truck.

On our way down and out of friendly lines, I racked my weapon ready to fire. That feeling still hadn't faded.

I could not overcome the sleep as it hit me like a ton of bricks, so I stood up; still that didn't help, so I grabbed some Tabasco sauce out of an MRE. I put some drops on my finger and rubbed it on my upper lip and then right under my eyes. Now my eyes started tearing up, but my plan had worked; I couldn't close my eyes even if I wanted to. I checked to make sure my driver and VC were still functioning then popped up and looked over my turret just in time to get back down. There had been a grenade thrown over the school wall that blew up just as I had ducked down.

I yelled stop at my driver, grabbed my M16, and stood back up.

Pivoting my body at the same time as I looked at where it had come from, I saw what couldn't be more than a five-year-old Iraqi boy bending down to pick up another grenade. I aimed in and yelled *awguf* which means stop.

Then I made a stand-up motion with the barrel of my rifle. He looked up like a deer in the headlights then stood up and stayed there for a second before trying to sprint away. By then though, the vehicle in front of me had dismounted and ran over to tackle him. We took him to his home which made the worst house in an American ghetto look like a mansion. The VCs dismounted and stormed the house like a bat out of hell. When they got inside, they detained the father and big brother. They continued to search the house and found three already-made IEDs just waiting to be planted and blown. They also found twenty-two AK-47 magazines fully loaded and a book on homemade explosives. Later on, we would find out that the father belonged to a terrorist cell called *Hab al Hit* and was the number 4 man on the battalion hit list.

We took off again to the supply point. It was a nice smooth ride from there, about ten miles of open desert. We made our way through the bottom of a waddie (creek). It was perfectly bumpy, and I hated going through the waddie because every time we went through it, I got thrown around like a rag doll. We went this way because it was the safest route. I would sacrifice safety for comfort any day.

When we arrived, I saw Gizmo, the puppy we had adopted. We had to give him away because our company gunny (gunnery sergeant) said he was "very unsanitary." It was a nice reunion; he had grown a lot since the last time, but he was still a puppy. His new owners played fetch with him, but when we pulled up, he stopped chasing the ball and came after us with a wet tongue ready for some loving.

I got off the truck, dropped my gear, then climbed in the backseat to get some rest, hopefully. The backseats were extremely tight; sitting back there resembled being packed in a can of sardines. I sprawled out across my turret stand, which is what I would stand on while in the turret. I couldn't get comfortable though, so I talked to my VC who couldn't sleep either. "Hey, corporal, you awake?"

"Yea, you can't sleep either?" Now he was one of my favorite NCOs (non-commissioned officers). I joked around with him all the time. If you asked me, he possessed much more leadership than I'd seen thus far. He knew that when it was time for business, it was just that, and when it was time to relax and have fun.

So I replied, "Yea, I'm sleep talking to you right now."

He laughed and said, "Okay, smart ass, say, has Leslie wrote you back yet?" Everyone I knew knew about her just from hearing me talk. It wasn't so much that I talked about her all the time; it was more being stuck out here for more than five months now. You get stuck with a group of people for so long you're gonna learn everything about them.

I replied, "No, I really don't expect her to; it'd be nice though. I thought she might at one time, but now I don't even care if she says 'You're psycho, stay away from me.' Anything to me would be better than nothing."

He laughed and said as he adjusted his glasses, "Yea, I know how you feel, kind of. My girl and I are fighting right now. You've talked to Jenna before, haven't you?"

"I think I've said hi a few times."

"Well, she keeps saying I don't talk to her enough." We looked at each other and laughed knowing the situation we were in. Then he continued, "Hey girl, sorry to break it to you, but I'm in Iraq and the bullets take up most of my time. I wanna call you; I just don't have the time. You know what I'm saying, Green?"

"Yea, man, I got you. That's the kind of thing that ticks me off—people and their ignorance to the obvious."

"Me too, me too. How long have you liked Leslie, that's her name right?"

I smiled thinking back to the million memories I had and thinking about the million more I hoped to develop. "Well, from the first day she walked into the school, so that's, what, three, maybe four years now. I wish I had a picture, you would think she's beautiful. Medium-long red hair, the most beautiful hazel eyes you've ever seen. I'm tellin' you you'd fall in love with her too. If you did, though, I'd have to kick your ass. You know the whole competition factor, nothing personal though."

"All you talk about is her, I'm sure I would. I think I do actually," he said while poking at me and laughing. Then he became serious again. "Just be sure when you get home you talk to her, whether she writes you back or not. I have a feeling she won't write, but she will think you're nice, then who knows where it goes."

"I sure hope so. What are you gonna do about Jenna?"

"I had planned on just letting her figure it out on her own. There's got to be more to it than me not talkin' to her enough."

"I don't know what to tell you, I guess that sounds good."

"Hey man I'm gonna try and catch some z's."

"Good luck." I was feeling tired myself and I wanted to go to sleep, but I couldn't shake the feeling I'd just acquired—the feeling of hopelessness.

I had finally found something—someone—worth fighting for. I was hopeless knowing there was nothing I could do to win her heart. I was 3,000 miles away and fighting a war. I couldn't talk to her, I couldn't make her laugh, I couldn't hold her in my arms when she was sad or just wanted to be held. She was home, probably working, maybe a thought of me crossed her mind every once in a blue moon. I thought to myself, *How can I care about someone so much, someone I talk to very rarely?* Then I realized that in life everyone has that special someone; and though she may not be that someone, she was for now, and that was good enough for me. As much as I loved to think about her, I hated it because it felt as if I were chasing the wind. No matter how hard I tried, I couldn't catch it. I could feel it, and it felt good, but I could never catch it. I sat in the back thinking for a few more minutes, then it was time to go.

We were on our way back now, just about to enter the city. There was a large crowd of people down in the souks (marketplace) today, shopping around getting gas and groceries. The people had just recently understood that we were there for them. They began to loosen up to us and feel more freedom in roaming their own town. I ducked down in the turret to take a drink of water. When I poked my head back up, we were in the city, and the streets were empty. The street being vacant was never a good thing, and I knew this. We were coming up on a Y intersection, and I began scanning around to find out what was wrong. Then the sleep hit me again. I dozed off dipping down into the protection of my shield. I woke back up not even a split second later; and before I could poke my head back up to start scanning again, the flash came, and I could see my life leaving me before the sound of the *boom* brought it back. If I had been standing, the blast would have decapitated me. I guess that was the way the good Lord was looking out for me. The dust hit me like a thousand little razors nicking at the skin, and I knew we were hit. I reached down, patted my legs. *Yep, they're still there.* Then I screamed a mute yell down in the cab, "Ya'll okay?" A few seconds passed and still no response, so I yelled again. This time, I got a response. My VC grabbed my leg, shook it, and yelled. All I could do was read his lips, no sound came out of his mouth. I could only hear the ringing in my ears, as another tone left that I would never be able to hear again.

His lips told me though, “Scan for secondaries.” I grabbed his arm letting him know I was okay and that I would start looking. Then I pointed at my ears to tell him I couldn’t hear him. I stood up and looked around for secondary IEDs then kicked him, letting him know I was jumpin’ out of the truck.

My hearing started coming back slowly; my ears still rang unimaginably loud. Everything I could hear, however, sounded like a whisper. As I was jumping out, I barely heard SSgt. Kay saying over the squad radio, “Vic 3, Vic 3, are ya’ll all right?” He couldn’t see us because the dust cloud was still as thick as molasses.

So to ease his nervousness, I came over the radio as I ran through the smoke to find the command wire saying, “Staff sergeant, we’re all good, I can’t hear you very well, but I’m out; VC and driver are good too.”

When the smoke cloud settled down, the rest of the marines in my vehicle got out. Cpl. Ski, meanwhile, had spotted the command wire, which was thin copper wire running along the backside of the curb. It was completely hidden from the side of the road we were driving.

When I saw him, I said, “I’ll go with you, let’s follow it.”

So we followed it. They had to be really close because the POO sight (point of origin) was only about 150 meters away. It was behind an old mud hut that looked like a storage building of some sort. We ran around the backside to avoid any kind of ambush they may have put up. The desert sand powdered up, like moon dust every time a boot hit the ground. They would do that a lot; that way, if they didn't hit you, or possibly even if they did, they could maybe get someone else with a trip wire. When we got to the sight, we split off to provide security on it. He posted up behind a huge rock full of craters, off of a wall littered with trash and random Arabic vandalism. I ran into an abandoned house not too far away. The house had no roof and burglar bars in the windows. The window I had chosen was extremely dirty and hindered my view but gave me the biggest, safe field of view out of the entire house, so I took the muzzle of my M16 and ran it through the window. It came down without any second hit. As I was scanning the area, I saw a man in black sweatpants, a white shirt, and a maroon turban take off in a dead sprint across the desert toward a cluster of houses. He was about 300 meters away, running across uneven terrain, which made it next to impossible to get an accurate shot off.

I took off out of my safe haven, running after him as I called over the radio, "Hey, I got a guy running to a group of houses. I'm in chase. Can I get some backup?" He had disappeared into a house now and I was about 100 meters away. When I finally got to the house, I sat outside for about ten seconds awaiting a cover man.

I was getting antsy, so I called back over the hook. "Where ya'll at?"

"Almost there, hold on." I thought to myself if I hold on any longer, this guy's gonna be gone. Do or die time, I decided. I took off with all I had and football style charged right through the door leading with my left shoulder. As soon as I got inside, a man was crossing the doorway. He wasn't the guy I was looking for, but the one I was after had come in this house.

So I immediately raised my muzzle, put it in his chest, and yelled, "Where the heck is he? Ali Baba came to this house."

He knew I wouldn't shoot him and that I was just exercising show of force, so he played dumb. "Mista, please, no Ali Baba." It was time to up my game a little bit. It was time to raise the threat level, so I took out a grenade, pulled the pin, and held the spoon. I held it up to my mouth and leaned in close to him, like I was going to give him a suicidal kiss.

Then I said in the calmest voice, "Where the hell is he?"

He looked wide eyed at me, like a raccoon, and started crying, then said, "Mista, he...over...there." He pointed to the next house with a shaky arm. I pushed him out of the way and ran out the backdoor. My support had finally caught up with me. We stacked on the door as we had been trained.

Right before we went in the house, I knocked out a window leaning in to look, then I yelled, "Go!" Then I charged into the house with the rest of the team. We searched the house and four other houses around it; we never found him.

The QRF squad came out to access the situation and rigged my vehicle for tow. The marines in my vehicle spread loaded ourselves in different vehicles throughout the convoy. We got dropped off at the FOB as the rest of the convoy pushed back to the supply point to get us a new vehicle.

When we got back to the room, I dropped my gear, then like a boxer's fist it hit me. My head pounded, I couldn't see straight. What I could see, though, was all colors, like looking through a kaleidoscope. My head hurt so bad it made me nauseous, I ran out of the room looking like I was drunk, I'm sure. The CO yelled at me. "Green, stop! What are you doing back here; I know you're supposed to be out right now?" He must not have heard what happened yet. I held up my hand in the stay back motion and ran to the corner of the sandbag wall then let it flow. I puked for what seemed like an eternity. I was trying to just stand and bend over to throw up, but my knees gave out and I ended up on all fours.

He ran over and said, "You okay?"

I looked up from my cow-like position and said, "Yes sir. We got hit that's why we're back."

"Well, I knew ya'll got hit, but I didn't know it was your vic." He checked up on me and the rest of us as we went our separate ways.

The next day, we were headed back to get more supplies; a lot of the supplies we had got had gone up in flames with the hit. We had just pulled out of the FOB and were headed to the south. I stood scanning the area and waving at the people or tossing candy out to the kids on the road. Out of the blue, I saw the same guy who had hit us yesterday. He was stupid and wore the same exact clothes. I yelled at my VC, "Stop, that's the punk ass that hit us yesterday, get 'im!" As he was jumping out to snatch the guy, I called a halt to the rest of the convoy and told them what I saw. Sure enough, it was the guy. He would later confess to it and reveal the location of some of his buddies and already emplaced IEDs. He was also part of the same terrorist cell as the last major guy we busted, *Hab Al Hit*. I would later be told that he was the number 8 man on the battalion's hit list.

It was Valentine's Day, and I had had permanent headaches drilled into my brain. I could feel it pulsing beneath my skull. The veins in my head, which normally didn't show, now showed clearly, like little rivers across my forehead. The constant explosions, whether they be controlled or enemy activated, had finally done a toll on me. I'd had three minor concussions now and been cut up a little bit more. Still I was fortunate; I hadn't had anything major wrong happen to me or the rest of the guys with me. I thanked God for this any time I had the opportunity. It had been about three weeks since we got hit, and the violence had been cut in more than half. We for sure had been winning the hearts and minds of the Iraqi populace. Life on the FOB was drastically changing for the better. We hadn't had a mortar attack in almost two months now. Ever since I got hit, there hadn't really been much going on other than the occasional pop shot. We finally got running water, which we hadn't had for the first four and a half months. It was nice to take an actual shower finally, instead of pouring icy water on yourself in the twenty-degree weather. It got a lot lower than that a few times. There were many times that we couldn't shower because the water bottles were frozen solid.

There was a patrol that had just left the wire; they were to set up a mobile COP (command outpost) for about a week. They would bounce around the city daily, never staying in one location too long to avoid enemy detection.

They were set up in a house for about four hours when we got the call we hated to receive. "Medevac 2 urgent surgicals, get your gear and get on the trucks." I had a few buddies in that squad; I prayed for the best but prepared for the worst. We pulled out about three minutes after we got the call, speeding through the town in and around corners, and got to the house they had been hit at about five minutes after we left.

I kept asking, "Who was it? Who got hit?" No one would give me an answer. It was a two-story white house, one of the nicer ones in the city. The burglar bars on the windows were red. There were no shades, and there were no windows; all had been shot out. They had been shot out since before today in previous skirmishes. What had happened, you see, was a grenade had been thrown through the window, or maybe it was an RPG, we still do not know for sure. They were on their downtime with a few guys up top on the roof providing security. The grenade made it through the burglar bars and landed in someone's lap. There were six people inside the room at the time and no one really heard it come in. The two sitting in the corner were the ones hit. It landed in one's lap and he rolled off, right before the blast. When the blast hit, it ripped through his legs like a cheese grater, leaving his limbs hanging by loose tendons and muscles, both legs gone just like that. The other marine had been sitting perpendicular to that marine and had taken the blast to the chest. They were both still alive and fighting for life. The corpsman, a freelance cameraman, and the rest of the marines applied first aid. They were all very heroic not giving in to emotion but doing their best to make sure the marines would live. The blood flooded the floor like a wet mop. As soon as we arrived, they had them on stretchers and ran them out to the medevac humvee. That's when I finally saw who one of them was—LCpl. Travis Boldson. He was a machine gunner like myself and had been a good friend of mine through my short career.

It chilled my bones, sending a shiver up my spine, hearing him say to his squad as he was carried away, "Stay motivated." Through all he had been through in the last ten minutes, he said, "Stay motivated!" They were words that would surely live in infamy. He had just lost his legs and was comforting the other marines when it was himself who should be comforted. Then the second stretcher came out with LCpl. Morrison. We had just talked the day before and taken a bunch of goofy pictures. His breaths were small and sometimes nonexistent. The corpsman kept clearing his throat of blood and performing moving CPR. His chest had been blown in, and there were about a million little pieces of shrapnel imbedded inside his chest cavity. He kept fighting for life, but as we were speeding over to the LZ (landing zone) for the helo's to pick them up,

God said to him, "Come home, my son," and with that, he left this world and reported into good St. Peter to stand guard, as all good marines do, at heaven's gates. They kept working on him, trying to bring him back all the way up until he got on the helo (helicopter), where he was pronounced dead. Meanwhile, the other corpsman working on Boldson tied tunicates and washed the wounds. He began to fade in and out as the adrenaline in his body began to fade into shock. They fed him IVs to help with the blood he had lost. They poured QuikClot (blood-clotting material) on his legs to keep the blood in his upper body rather than let it flow out and him bleed to death. He lived and is now in rehab in San Antonio, awaiting prosthetic legs, and will someday walk again. Both of these men are heroes; all the men there are heroes. It is with my utmost sincerity that I say this. They were awarded the Purple Heart on the 14th of February. This is why I cannot accept one. As the bird took off silently again, I found myself saying a prayer for them and their families. Happy Valentine's Day.

FEBRUARY 27

The chain of command had all the mounted sections rotating a blocking position for the past month and a half almost. One more of several unnecessary decisions that endangered marines lives—war and Politics...

Huh, don't belong in the same sentence, much less the same book. When you publicize a war, you kill more Americans than are necessary. Think logically for a second, if *CNN* or *Fox* says marines developed a new tactic, who is the next to find out about this great tactic that we have developed? The bad guys. Therefore, they are making the entire evolution of war fighting null and void.

We had to go to the same area over and over. We knew and had complained that there would be an IED there someday, and it would be big. The blocking position accomplished little if anything; every time we went there, we would talk about how nervous we were. We knew someone would get hit but didn't know who it would be. It was only a matter of time. I had gotten a new driver about a month ago because my last one had suffered a major concussion and could no longer drive. He went to the mounted section 5-2 and served as a dismounted sweeper. He was a great kid, LCpl. Astello. We disagreed a lot but he was one of the nicest guys I'd ever met. He had by far the biggest heart out of anyone I'd ever known.

5-2 had pushed out about 0530 to set up in the position, the same one we'd all been complaining about and were terrified of. My buddy Mike's vehicle split off to go to their parking position. They stopped and let the dismounts out to sweep the area. The job of the dismounts was to spot IEDs before the truck got to them. They had been up for about two days splitting day and night missions with us. LCpl. Astello was about five meters out in front of the truck sweeping. The sun had just poked up over the horizon, which this particular morning was very bland and plainly boring. There were no colors, no fresh air in the breeze; there wasn't a breeze at all really. It was still dark enough to dull the eyes' senses.

Meanwhile, we had just pulled into the FOB and were the acting QRF force for the day.

SSgt. Kay came in our room and gave us a motivating speech, saying, "Hey, I've been to Iraq three times, this is my fourth. You have done great things out here. You have all seen more than most people will ever see in their lives. You are here though. Your family is the marine to the left and to the right of you. Your family back home will be grateful and will tell you thanks for what you've done and the sacrifice you have paid to your country. Then they will go on about their daily lives. Your trophies, your awards, and your valor will be forgotten almost as fast as you earned it, but the man to your left and to your right will never let your memory fade. They will speak of your war stories, and you will speak of their valor and sacrifice. The only people who care what you've done are each other. I have seen brotherhood in every single one of ya'll. I am proud to be your convoy commander and couldn't pick a better group of marines to fight with. We got about two months left. Don't let down your guard now, keep up the good work, and go home, get your family home to theirs. Go to sleep, get some rest. We have a night operation tonight, detaining mission. We're gonna hit up about half the city, so we'll probably be out until tomorrow evening. Are there any questions for me?" We didn't have any, and he said, "Good. Make sure you all get some rest." With that, we started stripping down and getting comfortable in our racks.

Back at the blocking position, the trucks were maneuvering their ways out into the desert. They stayed off the road to allow civilian traffic to pass freely. I still don't know exactly what we were supposed to be blocking. Mike was standing up, scanning out in front of Astello. Their staff sergeant had given the order to get mounted back up. Astello had turned around, looked back at the horizon, then turned back to walk across the front of the truck. He took one more step, and he was gone; up in a cloud of dirt, shrapnel, and smoke. He had stepped on a pressure plate less than five meters in front of the truck. As it blew, it sent Mike to the back of the turret and sent his .50 cal into his lap. He picked up the gun, put it back up on the mount, then yelled down in the cab, "Cino, you all right?"

To which he replied, "What the hell!" Blood and body parts were sprinkled all over the truck, and on Mike's face. He whipped his face, peeling away the organs that littered it. About thirty meters away from the newly formed crater was LCpl. Astello's flak jacket which had kept his abdomen and chest cavity intact. His arms were barely there; they had been picked to the bone like a chicken wing. His head was there too, all cut up, and he was bleeding out of his eyes and ears. About ten meters from the upper half, they found a part of his leg, just the bone. Then came the worst part of the post blast, the police call or cleanup. They had to get out of their trucks and find all his gear and salvage what was left of him. While this was going on, the dogs started coming up to pick at the scraps that were left. They fended the dogs off until we got there to perform the medevac.

"5-2, 5-2, this is 5-1 over."

"Roger 5-1, this is 5-2. Send your traffic," they said in a rotten tone.

"We're pulling up to your position right now."

"Roger 5-2 out." We pulled up and loaded the body in the medevac truck then headed for the LZ to wait for the helo.

I along with my VC had a million things running through our minds. We hadn't been there, but we had seen the aftereffects, and he was our driver for the first five months. To see him like that ate at me. We were scheduled to go home in less than a month. You hated to see people die, but to have it be less than a month away is a kick in the balls.

There was nothing else that happened until we left back for the states. It ended on a peaceful note for the most part. We still had an occasional pop shot or grenade, but the violence had gone down by approximately 80 percent. We went over with nearly 200 marines and came back with about 160 due to KIAs and WIAs. Those men had shown true love; they had given their all and some of them their lives. They did this so that others may live, so that an oppressed people may know what freedom is someday. They did this so that the free may keep their freedom, which too many people take for granted nowadays. If they had one wish, I bet it would be for others to know their sacrifice and learn that freedom is not free. They would want people to respect and honor their sacrifice by showing daily that mankind has the ability to do great things if they will commit to it.

I still hadn't heard from Leslie and was nervous about seeing her, knowing that she got my letter and had never written back. I guess when I got home I would find out. It had plagued me more as the days got closer to my coming home.

WELCOME HOME

APRIL–MAY

IT WAS AROUND mid–April when we landed back in the states at our duty station. We had spent seven months in one of the most violent combat zones since the battle for Fallujah. It had been fun but also a real testament to a man's ability to tolerate extreme pressure and stress. No one should have to see what we saw, and most people have not. I thank God for this. We would have to step off the plane to a welcome home parade. As much as we appreciated it, getting to see our families and friends, we would have all much rather been doing it with everyone there. A few of our wounded made it to the parade; it was an honor to be in their midst. A hero's welcome for us, the survivors, and the less seriously wounded who had the ability to stay in the fight.

We stepped off as the roar of the crowd began; it reminded me of Friday night football games back home. I had grown up in a football community; more money went to the football team than it did to the school. I wouldn't see my family there because my duty station was 3,000 miles from my home. We walked down the steps slowly and with confidence. Our chins held high, though we all looked faded and beat. The emotions ran wild, wives getting to see their husbands for the first time in seven months. There were children seeing their fathers for the first time since birth, mothers and fathers seeing their sons, fiancée's seeing the groom-to-be, and the heroes taken out of the battlefront on crutches and wheelchairs. All were there to congratulate us. We shook hands and made small talk with families and friends. The banners were hung high in the hangar at the airfield. I walked down through the crowd of people and to the bus waiting to take us to our new barracks; I had no one to see. I said hi and thank you to a few people and shook hands with the wounded I could recognize. We were finally safe, on American soil. The air had never smelled so fresh. The scenery had never been so beautiful. There where mountains luscious and green with vegetation. The clouds followed the ridgeline, and a ray of sun poked through lighting up one part between two peaks revealing a portal to heaven. The bay reflected the sun and the water was clear blue with white sand. The palm trees stood tall and flawless. The ride back was only about a mile away. We could have walked, but the ride was nice and greatly appreciated. We could finally afford to be lazy, or at least for a little while. We turned in our weapons and sorted out our gear then reported to our rooms. There were fresh sheets and pillows; a pillow was a rare commodity in Iraq, you found them few and far between. The mattresses were firm and still intact. I lay down to relax after I opened my door to enjoy the fresh air.

Mike and I had made sure we would room together when we got back. That meant there would be mad parties in our room, and the first night back with no alcohol for seven months would be where we set the mood. He walked in the room and said, "Dude, guess who our third roommate is?"

"Who?"

"Third guy enter." It was my driver who had finished Iraq with me, LCpl. Traylor. A machine gunner also, he and I were good friends as well, even before Iraq. Now this definitely meant we would have the most hooked-up room in the barracks.

Then one of our buddies who had come back on the advanced party came to our room and said, "Don't buy any beer tonight, we hooked ya'll up. We got three kegs; there's one on all three decks. There's a beer pong tournament going on in the third deck lounge later; I expect ya'll to be there."

We all three looked at each other, smiled, looked back at him, and said as if cued by a choir conductor, "Hell, yea!"

I didn't know how much I would be able to drink because I was sure my tolerance had gone down a lot. We walked over to the little Chinese restaurant across the street and ate real food for the first time since we'd left for Iraq; it was amazing.

The rest of the night was a drunken haze, not much was remembered from that night. People who didn't drink made an exception to pour one out for the fallen. It started out fun but ended up on an emotional roller coaster. Everyone was talking and crying about buddies we'd lost and how much they wished it was them who had died or lost limbs. It was sad to talk about but necessary in order to get seven-month-long emotions off our chests. We didn't have to be at work until noon the next day, which was a Thursday, in order to account for the hangovers. We would have a speech by our BC (battalion commander) then be released on a 96 (four days off).

"How are we doing, gents?" the BC said.

The entire battalion in unison replied in a roar as loud as an earthquake "Oorahh!"

"Great, hope you all didn't try to drink seven months' worth of alcohol in one night, but who am I kidding? Seriously though, gents, listen up. You have made it through hell and come back. Don't lose your rank or, worse, life over something stupid. You have accomplished more in seven months than most people could hope to in a lifetime. Do not tarnish yours or this battalion's reputation by going out and being belligerently drunk. Your free night was last night, from hereon out, it's business. This battalion for those of you who don't know has received a citation from the president of the United States for nearly single handedly turning our AO (area of operations) in the Al Anbar province around. I know most of you don't know the stats and probably don't care, but you all cut the violence in more than three quarters. You allowed the Iraqi people a voice in a country where a voice gets you killed. When we started, our AO had less than ten Iraqi policemen. Now, at the end of our deployment, they have over 300. That in itself is a great accomplishment. Thank you, marines. You have all proved yourselves and need not prove it to anyone else. Take the time to get in touch with your families and let them know of the accomplishments you have done and been a part of. Lastly, gents, go out and enjoy your weekend. Monday we start training. We will be going back to Iraq for a second time here in a few months. When you get your new marines, treat them stern and fair and with the respect they deserve. Gents, I have nothing further."

The battalion sergeant major yelled in a voice that would put the fear of God in anyone. "Battalion, aten huhh!" We stood and then were released.

The words he had said were true, and I knew it—we all knew it. Still, though, for some reason, it didn't matter. It was not good enough. We could have single-handedly won the war and it still wouldn't have been fine. Nothing we did was good enough to bring back people from the dead; nothing was good enough to reattach legs and arms. Sure the Iraqi people were better off because of what we'd done, but most of the American people wouldn't know about, and a lot wouldn't even appreciate it because of their ignorance. To me, the Purple Hearts spoke louder than the accomplishments. I know the statistics didn't, but I don't care about statistics. Greater love hath no man than to lay down his life for another.

I had talked to my mom just the other day. We had been back for about a week now, and the air to me still hadn't gotten old. I was scheduled to go home soon along with the majority of the battalion on thirty days of leave. Anything more than twenty days was rarely heard of in the Marine Corps. I, along with two other buddies, were going to go home to Mike's house for three or four days to visit with him and his family. Then I would fly out from Chicago to go home. My mom and I talked for a while about how Josh and Trey were finishing up their school year and about how her and my dad's jobs were going. She asked about Iraq, and I lied again telling her it wasn't that bad. I hated to lie to her, but knowing I would have to go back, I didn't want her to worry. Then I asked about Leslie. I told her that she never wrote me back.

Then she told me, "Well, Leslie got your letter and thought it was very sweet, but she didn't know how to respond to it. She said all kinds of nice things about you, and she wrote you several times but couldn't find it in herself to send it out."

"Well, to me anything would have been better than nothing. I guess it's good she said that stuff though."

"Adam, I know how much you like her. I don't want you to get hurt, so I'm gonna tell you this. Leslie got a boyfriend about a month ago, and the rumor around town is that she's planning on marrying him. I don't know how true that is. Just be smart. You'll always be my baby. I like Leslie a lot, she's a great girl, but you're my son and I want only what's best for you."

It hit me hard. I was mad at myself for being in the military and for being gone to a foreign country. Maybe if I was home working construction or going to college, I would have had a chance. Then I realized everything happens for a reason and she may not have been the one for me. That thought, killed me inside. I would still talk to her when I got back just to ease the gap between us. I still wanted to be with her but in no way would I interfere with her relationship. I am not that kind of man. I would still continue to pray for her and her son every night. I wanted her to be happy; as much as it hurt me, I wanted only the best for her.

While I had been in Iraq on one of the safe bases, I had bought a green Iraqi soccer jersey; then back in the states, a maroon do-rag and some aviator glasses. My buddy Mike said, "No balls to meet my family like that." So whenever we all got down to the baggage claim, I walked behind the group and changed into my getup. They all got down there and met the family and told them I had been on a different flight and that my plane had just landed. I walked down the escalator in slow motion, adjusting my do-rag and glasses, then walked straight for the innocent family who would be braving four marines for about a week.

I tried my best to sell the part of being a thug; I had the gangsta lean and walked straight up to them, serious faced and said, "Say yo ya'll aint no where the Tompsons are, do ya." They looked at me like I was the biggest idiot they'd ever seen. Over at the baggage wheel, my buddies were standing there laughing hysterically, almost in tears. Then Mike came over and introduced me.

He said, still unable to contain his laughter, "Everyone, meet Adam Green. Green, this is my mom." I took my do-rag and glasses off, and shook her hand. Then I continued to meet everyone else. I think when I showed up, they knew they were in for a treat. We were going to party and drive them crazy. Mike had told me how cool his parents were; they were definitely that.

When we arrived at his house, his mom told us to get changed over into our uniforms for pictures. A little while and few pictures later, she broke the news to us that we were going to be in a welcome home ceremony. A fire truck pulled up to his front lawn to pick us up then drove us to the town hall. A lot of the townspeople were there; it was a small town of about 1,000 people. The mayor gave a little speech and then we talked to some older war veterans. There were some from Vietnam, some from Korea, and one from WWII. I always had great respect for veterans and would thank them for their service and their sacrifice. I did this because I know some of them were not paid the respect they deserved.

The next few days were great; we had a basketball tournament and a few BBQs. I loved cooking so I helped his dad out by flipping burgers at the grill. Come nighttime, it was time to go out and find a party. The weekend passed quickly and was full of events, but it was time for me to come home and face my demons. I thanked his family for allowing me to stay before I stepped on the plane to come home.

It was nice to be home finally. It had been about nine months since I had seen my family last. When we pulled up my driveway, seeing the place for the first time in a while was almost a new experience. The big oak tree at the front of my driveway stood sturdy and strong. The leaves rustled in the wind as they hung over the red entrance gate. The creek was dried up as we drove over the low water bridge. The fields of coastal grass flowed in the wind like ocean waves as the horses and cattle grazed to and fro. The pond looked a lot lower from where it had been before I left. The catfish were out today nipping at the top for insects. Catfish are a bottom-feeding fish, but for some reason, in my pond they would find their way to the top. Finally I was home. I grabbed my seabag and backpack, and walked up the steps in the house and to my room. Then Josh came in and said, "I bet I'll kick your butt in some Madden."

"Really, you think you can take the champ?" I said as I flexed.

"Well, you have been in Iraq for the last seven months, I figured you're probably a little rusty."

"Natural talent like mine doesn't fade overnight." It was a tough game, but as always I came out on top. I missed hanging out with my brothers so much; it was nice to see them again. They had grown so much, but then again I'd expected them to.

Wednesday night came. My mom had asked me to wear my dress blues for church. She said, "I wanna show off my baby." I was nervous about going because I knew Leslie would be there, and this would be the first time I talked to her since my letter. I didn't know what to expect. I ironed a few wrinkles out of my trousers then made the creases even sharper. I put my shirt on, clamped it with shirt stays, then pulled it tight and pulled my pants up slowly. I was dressed to impress. I wore my rank and ribbons proudly. What would Leslie think? "Mom, Dad, I'm ready. How do I look?"

"Like a bald sharp-looking marine."

"Thanks, but I prefer the term vertically challenged hair," I said as I splashed some cologne on.

When we arrived, the kids were outside playing on the playground. As I walked up the stairs, I put my military face on. I was hard, I stood tall, and I walked with confidence. When we got inside, I saw Leslie sitting in the back feeding her son. She was beautiful. I started to walk over to her before the entourage of people swarmed me. It felt like I was a celebrity with a million paparazzis surrounding me.

"Great to see you in one piece."

"Well, it's great to be in one piece." I talked to the people for a little while then dismissed myself and continued to hurdle toward my goal.

I said, "Hey there, how have you been?"

She looked up as if she'd seen a ghost, then smiled, and giggled, then said, "I'm great. It's nice to see you. How are you doing?"

I was nervous. I don't know if I showed it, but that confidence I'd walked in with rapidly started to crumble, and I felt more like a cream of wheat than a rock. Then she stood up to give me a hug. My knees were weak. Something was different about her, different in a good way, almost like I had a chance; that is what scared me. I'd always wanted and dreamed about this moment and had everything to say planned out like a map, but for some reason I couldn't find the words.

I replied in a less-than-confident voice. "I'm good. Is this the little guy?"

She beamed with elegance. "Yes sir, this is my pride and joy."

"Well, he is the cutest little man I have ever seen. Aren't you, buddy?" She placed her hand on my arm for a split second. I felt the warmth as it sent a chill down my spine.

"Thank you. So how was Iraq?"

"It had its ups and downs." I didn't really want to talk about Iraq so I tried to keep my answers about it brief and stay off that subject. I sat next to her, trying my best to hold a steady conversation.

She looked at me and said, "So, have you been enjoying your time home so far?"

"Yea, it's nice to be back. I get to spend some time with my brothers. Are you excited about graduating here in a few weeks?"

Her smile worn brightly, she said, "You know it. You better be there for it." I didn't know if this was just friendly conversation or if she really wanted me there.

I said, "Well, as much as I would love to, I have to be back about a week before your graduation, sorry."

Serious faced, she said, "Sure, you just don't wanna see me; I see how it is though."

"No, it's not like that at all."

She laughed then said, "I'm just kidding, I know how it goes."

Then the conversation got rough as she said, "You wanna go out this weekend? I want to talk to you. You know, about the letter." Wow, that was unexpected and threw the rest of my game plan out the window.

I replied, "Nothing would make me happier, but I already have plans, I'm going down to Houston for the weekend."

"Well, we gotta go out before you leave."

I smiled nervously. "Okay, that sounds good."

About that time, one of the youth teachers came up and asked me, "Hey, Adam, would you come talk to my class about Iraq next Wednesday?" I was glad for this little break; I could regain my composure for a second.

I told him, "Sure. How old are they so I know how to talk to them?"

"They're ten to twelve range."

"Okay, that sounds good." I continued to talk to Leslie for a little while until it was time to go to class. I had done it though; I had talked to her, and I could tell that there was something there. I couldn't place a finger on it, but all I knew is it had gone better than I expected—a lot better.

I had always tried to imagine taking her out but never thought it would really happen. Now that it was so close, I didn't know what to do. I would have done it this weekend, but my buddy in Houston was scheduled to go to boot camp the following week. Then I thought to myself, *She already has a boyfriend—no, a fiancé—what can I really say to change her mind? Can I even change it? Now I'm not the kind of man to mess around with other people's relationships, but I couldn't help wanting to interfere in some way.* I told myself I wouldn't, so I left it up to her.

Leslie had grown up on both sides of the fence. She knew what it was like to be poor, but she also knew what the upper class was like. Her dad had taken a job that required him to be gone a lot and for long periods of time, but the money he made was good. She enjoyed nice clothes if they were on sale and loved the scent of Clinique Happy lotion and lather. Before she had her son, she was a rebel, much like myself. She partied a lot and argued with her parents all the time. We were what I considered parallel; we walked the same paths that most likely would never meet. She had always had red hair, as had most of her family. After she had Tyson, she seemed to mature a lot and make better choices. Since I'd been in Iraq, I could see some more maturity building in myself. When the man who had gotten her pregnant found out, he made her feel like crap, not really anything new, though; told her it wasn't his and he wanted nothing to do with her or the kid. He would tell her she was worthless and would never, and could never, do better than him. The sad thing is she believed him for the longest time, and her brain housing, the way she thought, proved the saying "nice guys finish last." Almost all of her boyfriends, though she hadn't had many, had treated her generally the same way. I felt bad for her and wanted to prove to her that not all nice guys have ulterior motives. That experience, whether she wanted it to or not, would always haunt and lurk in the back of her mind. She would always question every man after, review them up and down, sometimes even look too far and find reasons that made no sense to anyone, including herself, not to trust them. She was a beautiful young woman both inside and out trying to make it in a harsh world with a child. Her son could have easily been the next Gerber baby.

The next time I saw her was the following Sunday, and I would have to leave the next. My time was fading fast;

if anything was going to happen, it would have to happen soon. That Sunday when I saw her, I walked over to her after the service had ended and started a conversation. "Hey, Leslie, how are you doing."

"I'm awesome. You haven't talked to me in a while." She said this like she had been truly disappointed and wanted me to.

So I replied, "Sorry, I've been kind of busy. You sound upset."

"Upset about what?"

"You sound like you wanted to talk to me."

She smiled and laughed then said, "Well, I told you last time I wanted to talk to you, you have just been avoiding me." I was taken aback because this was somewhat true.

I said, "Leslie, your right, I'm terrified of talking to you. I get nervous every time I see you."

She said like she thought I was joking, "Yea, I know. I'm like the boogie monster. I'm sooo scary."

With a nervous laugh, I said, "No, I really literally have the butterflies in my stomach right now. No, I take that back; they're everywhere now." Her already beautiful smile got even bigger and more elegantly seductive. Not the kind of sexual seduction, but almost as if she had been wanting me as long as I had wanted her.

Then she said, "You are so sweet. I really want to talk to you some time about the letter you wrote me. What are you doing tomorrow night?" I had plans to go out and party with my buddies, the colleges had just got out for the summer and this was supposed to be one of the biggest college parties of the year.

As one of my buddies had said, "One for the record books." To me, though, this was a once in a lifetime opportunity. I could party any time I wanted. If I didn't go out with her tomorrow, though, I may never get the chance to go on a date with an angel again. I had been so afraid in Iraq about not getting to talk to her, which made the answer crystal clear for me.

So I said, "Well, tomorrow night I have plans with a beautiful redhead to go to Chili's."

"Oh, yea, do you mind if I tag along?" She said smiling with a slight look of excitement.

I said, "Well, I don't know; I'll ask her real quick."

I paused for a moment then said, "Do you mind if you tag along with me to Chili's tomorrow night?"

She laughed then said, "I'd love to. Pick me up at 6:00. How'd you know I like Chili's?"

"I guess I just made a snap decision, and it was the first restaurant that came to mind."

"Well, I love Chili's, and it's been a long time since I have been there. So I guess I'll see you tomorrow?"

"Definitely!"

I turned to go to my truck, and as I was turning, she grabbed my hand and pulled me back around then said, "So, I'm not gonna get a hug now?"

That sent my heart to the sky, and I said while I was hugging her, "Oh, sorry. I told you I get the butterflies." She giggled then turned around to leave, as did I before I realized I didn't have her number.

"Hey, Leslie, I just realized I don't have your number to get a hold of you." She turned around and tripped right into my arms. I tried not to laugh but couldn't hold it.

"Okay there, meanie, that's not how you're gonna get my number." She said this after she herself got done laughing hysterically. Then as she pulled herself back up, she gave me her number; we said good-bye again then went our separate ways.

I held my cool walking back to my truck with gelatin legs and a heart that if it beat any faster would have a heart attack. I got in and sat there for a few minutes thinking how on earth a man could get this lucky. I stared at her number. I know it sounds foolish, but I had always dreamed of this moment. That number was a stepping stone upon which I'd hoped many more would come. The drive home wasn't but a mile and a half, but I took my time weaving in and around the corners until I got home. The grill was started, and when I walked inside, my momma looked at me then said, "You all right? You look a little dumbfounded?"

"Well, I am. Leslie asked me out tomorrow night. I always saw it happening, but when it finally did..."

"You've never looked like this with the girls in the past."

She said with the same confused look I had, then I replied, "Yea, I know. There's something about her though."

"Well, I know how much you like her, but doesn't she still have a boyfriend?"

"I didn't even think to ask; she didn't act like it. I'll find out tomorrow, and if she does I'll make her chose, because I can't do that to him."

My mom smiled then said, "Well, that is very mature of you. For now, though, you got some steaks to cook." I loved grilling, and as I did it, I took some time to gather my thoughts.

After we ate and all was said and done, I walked out to the dock to watch the sun set. We had made a dock out of 2 × 4's and plywood for evenings such as this. I lit the tiki torch we had out there and sat in the old rusted iron rocking chair we had put out there for an antique theme. The tree behind me provided a nice addition to the theme; it had been burned a few years before in a field fire, but it refused to die. It stood tall, and the look said, "I'm old but I'm not going down that easy." The sun began to fade an orange to purple sunset; the sun itself reflected off the water and was chopped and broken by the little waves in the pond. The field behind ours looked as if it were on fire due to the way the sun hit the grass. The wind blew smoothly against me; it tingled the hairs on my arms as I swayed back and forth. Today was a beautiful day—a magical day that I would never forget. Though nothing really happened, not even Alzheimer's could take it away from me. When the stars finally came out, I decided to call it a night. I went to bed, and three hours later I was in a cold sweat as I was woken up by my brother.

He said I was screaming then would say, "Stop!" and scream again, which had woken him up.

I sat up for the next hour or so thinking about the past and thinking about the future. I fell asleep thinking about Leslie and our date. I slept sound and woke up refreshed. Just as it had been a beautiful night, it was a beautiful morning as well.

FIRST DATE

MAY 17

MONDAY MORNING WAS slow, my little brothers still had school, and I was home. So I figured instead of making them wait out for the bus, I would take them, and while I was there I could visit some of my old teachers. I know a lot of people don't like their teachers and would never go visit with them after they graduated. I think though, second to your parents, teachers mold young men and young women into the people they become. So I swung by and talked to all the ones I could find for a few minutes apiece. They would all ask the same questions: "So how was it?" or they would say, "We're so proud of you." It was always nice to hear, but I'm just your average Joe; I am no one special. When I die, my family is the only ones who will remember me, and that'll only last for a few generations. No one will remember my war stories. It would be nice, though, to defeat the overwhelming presence of ignorance that grows upon everyone eventually.

I came back to the house and did the dishes when a hunger struck me like a baseball bat. I looked around the pantry and the refrigerator and came to the conclusion that there was nothing worth eating. So I decided to call my mom and said, "Do you wanna go to lunch in thirty minutes?"

I could tell she was having a busy day by listening to the rustling of papers in the background and the sound in her voice when she said, "Yea, I could use a break."

I went out to my truck to find that in the middle of the Texas summer heat, my air conditioning had gone out. Hopefully later, Leslie wouldn't mind taking her car, or being miserable the whole time in mine. I didn't really think she would care either way. The way her voice was and the way she was talking to me, I think she just wanted to see me. I had done something, or was she just toying with my emotions? No, there's no way; she wasn't that kind of girl.

I dropped my truck off at the school where my mom worked. Then I rode with her over to Brody's Burger Shack on Adams Street. It was a hole-in-the-wall restaurant but had the best food for the buck in the area.

I asked my mom as soon as I got in her car, "So you sound like you're having a busy day?" She drove with her hands at 10 and 2, and sat close to the pedal.

She replied while staring intently at the road. "Yea, I have all the TAF paperwork due at the end of the week. I'm probably going to have to bring it home and work on it in the evening. There's a lot of it." This is why I was in the marine corps infantry; I hated doing paperwork or being behind a desk. I knew my chances of that kind of work were slim to none being a machine gunner.

I replied to her, "Is there anything I can do to help?"

With a stressed-out laugh, she said, "No, you have a date tonight and I want you to enjoy your time while you're home. So what do you have planned for tonight? Anything special?" She asked as we got out and went inside to pick our table.

"Well, I don't really have a plan. I think I'm just gonna play it by ear. I don't want to interfere if she still has a boyfriend, but at the same time, I don't want to let her just slip away. I can't just let her go without even trying."

"Oh, I know, sweetie. Adam, I know how much you like her and how long you've liked her; you need to just take it slow. I don't wanna see my baby get hurt."

My mother is a very sweet lady, not just to me but to all the people around her. She is in the public service business, and I think she likes it. I know she hates the paperwork but helping kids is her cup of tea. Her face would light up anytime we talked about the kids she worked with. I started to learn a lot about them. Kasey was a sweet little blonde girl who had trouble in math. My mom had helped her to where she got a B+ on the last test. Another kid named James had Down syndrome. She stopped some bullies from picking on him the other day. She had cried that night she came home thinking how people can be so cruel. Sometimes, I felt as if I'd worked with her and had a relationship with the kids the way she did. We talked for a while longer about Leslie and just life in general. Then I left and went to the mall to buy some different cologne. I like the stuff that makes you smell like an old man, but yet still modern. Something that says "I'm mature but I still like to have fun." I couldn't make up my mind, so I asked the lady behind the counter what she liked for men that fit my description. She said in a smart-aleck voice, "Well, Old Spice kind of nails it on the head, don't you think?" I decided to just gaff her off; I wasn't a big fan of people who were rude, and that's how she struck me. All in all, I just called my dad and asked if I could use some of his.

It was about 4:30, and I needed to leave by at least 5:30 to get to her house on time. She used to just live right down the road, but since I'd been in Iraq she had moved. I started getting ready; I shaved a goatee, which in the military I wasn't allowed to have. I shaved without shaving cream, out of habit. Out in the field, you never know if you're gonna have shaving cream or enough water to even use it. I also liked the way it made my face feel rugged and rough. I then thought about shaving my chest but decided if she didn't like it, oh well, that's her problem. I wasn't planning on getting to that tonight; and if it came to that, well, I wouldn't let it come to that. I did not want a one-night stand, and she wasn't that kind of girl anyway. I don't even know why I had thought that, so I just swept it under the bridge. I believe that sex before both are ready ruins relationships. Even if both parties are ready, it can still easily ruin them. I then moved on to the teeth; I had the same routine every time—brush the top for a minute, then the bottom for a minute, then alternate for a minute. I didn't have the whitest teeth but I liked to try, or at least have a fresh-feeling mouth. I got a shower, dried off, then put on the clothes I had already laid out on the bathroom towel bar. I wanted to look good, but not like I was trying too hard, so I went for a pair of board shorts and a pearl-snap shirt. They didn't really match, but then again I never could match; God didn't bless me with that gift. He had blessed me with too many other things already, like going bald at sixteen, or helping make up my mind to get out of the house about a month after my eighteenth birthday. With gifts like these, who needed to match? I squirted on some cologne, probably a little too much, then popped some gum in, told my folks and brothers bye, and headed out. I patted my dog, Zeke, on the head and told him I'd be home later to talk to him. He was a good listener.

As I pulled out of my driveway and drove off, I thought to myself. I thought about what I would say in certain situations; nothing was clear though. This night, no matter how it went would be a dream come true for me. What was she thinking? Was she still with Brandon? These questions lurked in the back of my mind like a panther in the dark. I knew Brandon; we used to play Texas Hold'em together. He was a great guy, and I hated the fact that he was as cool as he was. I hated the fact that I was moving in on his girl. I felt guilty, but at the same time I knew if I ever wanted to be with her, I might have to go out of my comfort zone; I might have to do something wrong. I was in a great mood for the situation but still nervous. When I finally got to her street, I gave her a call to make sure I was in the right area and headed toward the right house. As I pulled up and parked, I sat out there for a second, regaining the composure I never had when I was around her. Now or never, and I walked to the door.

Knock, knock, knock! I could hear her running down the stairs, and when she opened the door, the unexpected happened. I hugged her before I said hello, and she returned my embrace. The lines and curves of her body pressed against mine. We held the hug for a little too long for her to have a boyfriend still. I didn't want to be a rebound guy, but if I wasn't that, I may not be anything. She was wearing a skirt about halfway to the knees; it was blue polyester. She had a lime-green spaghetti strap on; the whole uniform fit her body perfectly. I said, "Hi, how was your day?"

With a smile, a giggle, and a soft squeeze to my arm, she said as she let go, "Too long and pretty busy."

"So, are you gonna leave me standing out here, or can you show me the new house?"

"You're mean would you like to see the house? When are we leaving?"

I smiled. "Yes, and as soon as I see the house and get to say hi to your mom." She walked me through the house, and it was beautiful, very spacious and open.

She yelled down the stairs. "Mom, Adam wants to say hi."

I looked at her and said, "I can go down and say hi; you don't have to bring her up here."

"Oh, I know, but I still have to show you my room." Her room was huge. The crib was in the corner; the bed was a twin and placed strategically in the middle of the room. I watched Leslie's soft features beneath the amber light and caught my breath. She was beautiful, an angel in the midst of this violent earth. She let herself fall back first on her bed, immediately bouncing back up. I said hi to her mom and talked for a little while about Iraq with her, then we left.

We took her car, much nicer than my truck, and it had AC. On our way, I asked in the middle of a conversation. "I hate to ask, but I heard you had a fiancée?"

"No, well I did, but I prayed about it, and well, I just didn't love him. We're broke up now though."

Trying to stay safe, I said, "Sorry about that."

She laughed and said, "Don't be. He wasn't the right one. I'm not even upset about it. I normally got kind of sad after a breakup, but not after him. To tell you the truth, I don't even know why we dated. Honestly, even if we were still together, I still wanted to talk to you about the letter."

"Okay, good, because I was wondering if he knew about this."

"Knew about what?"

"Us going out tonight?"

"Adam, we would have done this anyway." I thought the conversation was moving a little too fast and didn't really want to talk about the letter just quite yet. I knew that the way we were talking, it would come up soon, so I decided to change the subject.

"So what are you planning on doing after high school?"

"Well, I wanna go into real estate. I already have it all planned out." She was so proud of herself, which in turn made me proud of her too.

"Well, that's good that you know what you wanna do."

"What are you gonna do when you get out?"

"I'm not exactly sure. I've thought about staying in, but if I get out, I think I'll go to college just for a degree in whatever and then never use it. I don't know, maybe be an English teacher or open up a hunting and fishing store. Basically, wherever the road takes me, I'll go. You can't fight destiny, and I believe everything happens for a reason." She smiled intently and glanced at me. The gleam in her eyes told me I was saying the right things. I wasn't trying to say the right things though; I was simply just being me. No point in being a different person only for her to find out later on down the road that I wasn't who she thought I was.

The sun was going down as we pulled into the parking lot. The crisp evening air blew swiftly bringing her scent to my nose. I breathed in the beauty and looked up to the heavens as if to thank God for this day. As we walked up, we brushed hands—both too afraid to reach around for the hold, but the thought was going through both our heads. We got a booth seat with a parking lot view; not the most romantic seat in the house, but then again, romantic was never really my thing. I thought of what to talk about but nothing really came to my mind. Once again, I had planned it all out, and nothing. What was it about her that completely infatuated me? I looked at her and thought how lucky I was and how long I'd wanted to be in this very position. I was sitting right across from the memory that had gotten me through the rough times in Iraq. Finally, I decided to break the awkward silence. "It's been a while since I've been here."

"Yea, me too. The last time I came here was with Nic, and we just drank the whole time. That was probably a year ago."

"So, what are you gonna get? I think I'm gonna have the Cajun steak."

With a look of excitement, she said, "The old-fashioned burger looks good, I'm gonna have that."

She paused for a moment then looked at me with intent eyes and said, "I know you've been trying to beat around the bush. Why are you afraid of talking about the letter you wrote me?" I was put on the spot now; I had no choice but to talk about it. I could feel my heart trying to beat its way out of my chest.

Of the million things I could have said, and all would have been true, I went with. "Leslie, I'm scared of what you think, I'm scared of you knowing how I feel. I have liked you for several years and have always been afraid to tell you how I felt. I wrote you that letter to inform you. I didn't even send it out because I was too scared. My buddy Mike took it and sent it because

I had already written you about a thousand others and thrown them away. I'm scared because I don't know how you feel about what I wrote, about me. You know practically everything about me, and I know little to nothing about you." Then there was silence. I had blown my one and only chance, I knew it. She had ducked her head while I had been talking. At that specific moment in time, I could feel it though—something good, something about her, the warmth of her thoughts was burning my entire being. It was almost as if I had turned the tables and made her nervous now.

She picked her head back up and in a watery voice said, "I have never got a letter like that before. I've never heard anything like that before. Adam, did you mean it? Did you mean what you wrote, or was it just because you were in Iraq and didn't know what to think?" I looked deep into her eyes as if searching for her soul.

And in the smoothest, most convicting voice, I said, "Every single word. I meant every word. I wrote it because, like I said in the letter, I wasn't sure if I'd get the chance to tell you. I wanted you to know how I felt in case I didn't make it back. Now that I can tell you, it's a weight off my shoulders. If you want me there, Leslie, I will be there... I can't believe you haven't got a thousand letters like that; you're beautiful both inside and out." My feelings had been laid on the line. It felt good, and at the same time I was still terrified. Why?

"That letter was the sweetest thing I've ever heard. You are an amazing guy. How can you write things like that, things that cut to the core with no effort? Why do I have the feeling that every word you say is true?"

I smiled shyly. "Because, I got nothin' to lie about..." I let the words sink in then continued, "I just write the thoughts as they cross my head. Also, after writing a thousand of them, I'd hope it sounds good. Leslie, I just wanted you to know how I felt, so I wrote it down. Why didn't you write me back? I would have rather got a hate letter than nothing. It drove me crazy after a while."

Her beautiful smile shined once more. She looked at me the same way I looked at her and smoothly said, "Adam, I did write you back. I wrote you five different letters. At the time when I got the letter, I didn't feel the same. I wasn't ready for a relationship. I wrote that the letter meant so much to me, and even though it found its way into my heart, I still wasn't ready. I knew you were in Iraq and didn't know how you would take it; I didn't want to hurt you. I'm glad I didn't send it out now though." Well there was the answer I was looking for, we would just be friends from here on out.

I tried not to sound upset as I said, "I'm a big boy. I would have rather got something than nothing. If you weren't ready for a relationship, why did you date Brandon?"

"I dated him because I was insecure. He was there and I thought I was ready, but I wasn't. I realize that now."

"Why are you glad you didn't send it?" Her face was beautiful, the way the light hit it. Her cheeks, her eyes, her nose all smoothly shimmered. She always smiled, but I could clearly see a difference in the smile she had now than the one she normally had.

She said, "I'm glad I didn't send it because if I had, we wouldn't be here tonight." It was apparent what she was trying to get across. She no longer felt as she had written. She was ready for a relationship. She was ready for me. I was ready too; I'd been waiting for years for this moment, and it was lingering right in front of me. I wanted it so bad, but instead I thought, *Take it slower, take it slower, not tonight.*

So I did, as I said, "Well, I'm glad we're here too. How's your burger?" Maybe it wasn't the smartest choice of words, but it would slowly change the subject.

She said, "It's amazing. How 'bout yours?"

To lighten up the mood, I said, "Well, I have a steak not a burger, but my steak is good. It's not quite bloody enough for me though."

"Eww, how do you eat steaks like that? I like mine well done."

I kind of laughed as I said, "Well, I like mine still mooing."

"That's gross. Hey, after we're done here, can we go to the mall? I have to return some clothes."

"No, I don't want to go to the mall...Yea, of course we can go." I didn't have much time left at home and wanted to spend every waking moment with her.

She giggled and said, "Good, that's what I thought."

Tonight was amazing, and it was tough to take it slow but I knew I would have to. I was not only doing it for her, I was doing it for myself. We talked for a little while longer then I paid the bill, which she tried to pay, but I wouldn't let her. I wasn't rich, but she had a child and needed every dime, and I didn't think it was right letting her pay for it. Then we headed to the mall.

It was a full moon and the stars were shining bright tonight. The clouds glowed as they majestically rolled into the scene. We went into the store to change out the clothes. She asked me to help her find something cute. This was not my forte; I had no sense of fashion.

She said as she purposely brushed against me, "What do you think about these shirts?"

She was holding up a horizontally striped blue-and-white spaghetti strap, in front of a green-and-white one.

"I guess it would look good, but I think you could wear something crap brown and still look good."

She held it up to her body and looked at me as if she wanted me to judge her, then twisted her hips to look in the mirror behind her.

"I think it's cute." I liked the way girls could go from intellectual to a blonde ditz in a matter of seconds whenever they were around clothes, that's what I thought was cute.

She turned back to face me and asked, "So what do you think?"

"I don't know, I think you look good. The clothes do too, I guess."

She laughed and said, "Well, you're no help; I'm gonna get it." I tried to get for her as a late Mother's Day present, but she wouldn't let me. We walked back outside as the rain started to fall. She started to take off for her car, which she had strategically placed at the back of a next-to-empty parking lot. I was lax and enjoying the feeling of the rain on my skin, but in the end I decided to run and catch up.

The ride back was slow; the rain was pouring now. The moon and stars still shined bright in spite of the weather conditions. She turned on the radio and said, “Listen to this song; it’s the story of my life.” As the song played, it made me angry—angry at all her past boyfriends. I don’t know who sang it or what it was called.

It said, “Do you feel like a man when you push her around? Do you feel better now as she falls to the ground?”

I asked her, “That’s horrible. Why would you allow yourself to be treated like this?”

“I thought I was in love. I thought that’s what love was, and then I got pregnant and he left. It was tough at first, but now I’m glad. Him leaving was the best thing for me and for Tyson.”

“Leslie, you deserve so much better than that.”

She looked at me and smiled. I looked at her, holding her eyes in mine. This wasn’t the smartest thing to do while driving in inclement weather. She ran off the road and *pop*, a tire blew out. I had a flashback for a split second thinking I had just been blown up, white knuckles grasping whatever I could grab. Sudden loud noises seemed to do that to me now. She kept control of the car though, slowly driving back onto the shoulder of the road.

She screamed in frustration, "Crap!" then put the car in park.

She took her hands and squeezed the steering wheel tightly, about to cry, until I laughed.

I placed my hand on hers, laughed, and said, "It's okay."

I tried to ease her nervousness as she began to laugh hysterically. We stared at each other and began to laugh together, sitting inside the car with the rain pounding all around.

When we finally regained our composure, I said, still laughing, "Don't worry, I'll change it. Where's your spare?"

"It's in the trunk. Do you want some help?"

"No, I want you to stay dry; I'll take care of it."

I got out, pulled the tire out, and began to go to work. It was the rear passenger tire that had blown. I sat there getting pelted by the rain. *This was the perfect first date,* I thought sarcastically. Meanwhile, she had gotten out of the car and walked around. She was staring at me. The rain made my shirt tight on my body, revealing the cuts and curves of my muscles. I wasn't the most fit guy, but I did have great physical fitness because of the marine corps. I worked steadily wrenching away at the nuts and bolts, beads of water forming and rolling off my head. She came up behind me, knelt down, and placed a hand ever so softly on my shoulder, sending a chill down my spine. She placed her other hand on my bald head and began caressing. I turned around slowly with the tire halfway off and stood up. I grabbed her hand, pulling her up. Her hair was soaking wet and dripped as I slowly moved it away from her face. I grabbed one arm and held it out to the side as the rain pounded down all around us. I placed my other hand in the small of her back and slowly started swaying side to side. We didn't speak. I moved one foot then the other as we held each other tightly. She placed her head against my chest, and I placed my chin, the goatee stubbly from not shaving, lightly against her head. We rocked back and forth, spending what we had both waited an eternity for in just one moment. She lifted her head and stared into my eyes with intent and burning desire. I locked the gaze as we breathed each other's breaths. The air of young matured hearts beating wildly was heavily inhaled. I leaned in for a kiss as did she almost like we'd thought about it at the same time. We made the first move at the same time. Then it hit me—*don't!* Don't kiss her; it's the first date. Don't kiss her. You respect her, savor her, and wait.

So an inch from her, I sighed and said, "Sorry, I can't. I gotta finish getting that tire on."

She looked at me as if to say "Am I not good enough?"

Without her saying a word, I replied. "Leslie, as much as I would love to kiss you tonight, and believe me, I do, I can't because you mean more to me than that, and whether or not you think I need to show you that, I think I do. Don't be offended. I have dreamed of this moment for a long time; hell, I've dreamed of the whole evening for a long time. Out of respect, Leslie, not tonight? You understand, don't you?"

She had turned her head in shame, still hinting that she didn't understand, then looked at me. I think she was crying, but the rain made it tough to tell, and said, "Yea."

As the first visible tear hit my arm, I said, "Leslie, look at me."

I softly grabbed her chin and brought it up and said again, "Leslie, look at me. You are beautiful, even when you're sad, it's cute. Like those clothes we bought today. What do you say we get out of here? Go back and get warm."

She wiped her eyes with no avail; the rain still poured. She then forced a smile and said, "That sounds good, warm is nice. No one has ever done that for me, no one has ever treated me so nice. You're not like other guys."

I smiled and kissed her on the cheek then said, "Well, I'm not just another guy. I am what I am, and that's all I can give. You wanna help me finish this tire, seeing as we are both already soaked."

She laughed and said, "I would like nothing more than to just kiss your face right now, but if a tire changing is all I'm gonna get, I'd love that too...You are so sweet, Adam."

We worked together closely, but neither of us tried a second move. I couldn't ask for a better first date. It was truly breathtaking, so monumental that no words could ever explain. When we got done with the tire, we both stood up and faced each other. I reached for her hand and pulled it around me, and once again we held each other close. She lightly caressed my back as I softly ran my rugged fingers through her hair.

I softly whispered to her, "You are beautiful, and you have no idea how much tonight means to me. No idea how much you mean to me. I don't want to ever do anything to mess that up...You are beautiful."

Then we just sat there for a while, rocking back and forth, keeping each other warm, our embrace soaked up the evening as well as the rain.

The ride back was quiet, with very minimal conversation. It was necessary, however. Both of us needed to regroup and gather our thoughts. I had dreamed of tonight for a while. She, however, well, I was just a new flame who had left a spark. She knew me only as a friend before, as did I, but I had always wanted more; she had not. This was tough for me to grasp because what had happened tonight spoke of an entirely different book. I knew, though, I needed to take it slow. She would fall fast; I just didn't want it to be too fast. I knew if we went too fast, most likely we wouldn't work out. That was the last thing I ever wanted. I was playing no games with her, I cared too much. I had done it before. I was never a prick or abusive in any kind of way, but I somehow knew how to get my way. I didn't and would not ever do this to her. I wondered what she was thinking, I thought of so much she could be thinking then decided it best to just not worry about it and let the cards lie where they fall.

We pulled into the drive as the rain slowly started to subside. Both of us were still soaked to the bone.

She looked over at me and asked with a smile, "Would you like to come in, or do you have to be home at a certain time?"

I laughed and said, "I'm a marine, my momma's not gonna give me a curfew. But seriously, if I come in, what are we gonna do?"

"We can talk and play with Tyson; he's normally up for about another hour. I think it's cute that you call your mom 'momma.'"

I smiled then said, "I'd love to then."

When we walked in, her mom walked by and glanced at us then turned back to look again and said, "What happened to ya'll?"

We looked at each other and said "flat tire."

Then her mother replied, "Oh, well, did ya'll at least have a good time?"

I said "Yes, ma'am, I had a blast. Leslie is an amazing young woman."

She smiled and said, "That's why I like you, because you know just how to kiss my butt."

I knew she was joking, so I sarcastically returned with, "That's why I came in wet, because I know you like the wet kisses."

Then Leslie butted in and said, "Mom, can I have him back? We're gonna go upstairs and play with Tyson."

Her mom laughed and said, "Someone's jealous. Adam, no later than midnight."

I smiled and said, "Yes ma'am, no later than tomorrow at midnight."

"Okay there, smarty pants, ya'll have fun; you know when to be gone."

"Yes, ma'am."

Upstairs, we played some soft music, trying to tire Tyson out. He was so cute, a chubby baby with a chubby face and baby-blonde hair. He wasn't crawling yet, but his little arms and legs didn't know that. He tried and tried then began to whine when he saw us laughing at him. I low crawled over to him then pushed him over and tickled him. He would squeal and laugh as Leslie sat back watching us.

She would smile and laugh, then tease him telling him, "Come here, baby, come here."

I picked him up and put him on my back then low crawled back to momma.

I rolled him off my back and lay on my side then said, "Go to momma."

I locked eyes with her and said, "You are amazing."

She smiled then said with a nervous but soothing voice, "Thanks."

I looked at the clock—11:50. I hated to leave but knew it was the best thing to do.

I smiled at her then said, "I should be going now. It's almost midnight. Thank you so much for tonight."

She smiled and said, "Yea, hold on a second and I'll go down with you."

She grabbed Tyson and put him in his crib, then turned on his little crib display. She turned on his little baby monitor to hear if he started crying. Then she said, "You ready?"

"Yup."

When we got out to my truck, I pulled down the tailgate and said, "You wanna sit with me for a minute before I leave?"

She laughed and said, "All this time I took you for the nervous shy guy. Sure, I can sit for a minute."

I laughed a nervous laugh then said, "When I said 'thank you for tonight,' I meant it in two different ways; the way that it sounds because I had a great time and wouldn't trade it for the world. Then I also meant 'thank you for opening me up,' you seemed to somehow be able to break me out of my shell."

She laughed then said, "Well, I've never felt like I feel now on a first date before, thank you."

"Well, how do you feel right now?"

I knew this was the wrong question to ask and knew she wouldn't answer it.

She hesitated then said, "Well, I feel good."

We sat there for a moment, enjoying the night and the stars before she said again, "What was Iraq like?"

I couldn't talk about it; the only people I talked to about it were my brothers in arms, people who had been there and done that. The civilian population would never understand; I know she just wanted to know more about me, but that was one thing I wouldn't talk about.

So I said, "Hell," and just left it at that.

She looked at me and smiled then said, "I understand it was rough for you, and you probably don't want to talk about it, so I'm not gonna force the subject. If you ever want to talk to someone about it, though, you can talk to me about it."

I never would talk about it, so I just responded politely and said, "Thanks that means a lot."

I hopped off the tailgate and said, "I should probably get going, it's getting late. Do you wanna come over for dinner tomorrow?"

She smiled, still sitting there, and said, "Would your parents be okay with it if I brought Tyson?"

I smiled and said, "I know my mom would try to steal him from you."

Then in a sarcastic voice, I said, "Of course, you can bring your son."

She laughed and said, "You're a dork. What time do you want me to come over?"

"Whenever you want, the sooner the better."

"4:00 sound good?"

"Yes, ma'am. My mom gets off at 4, so that would be perfect. See you tomorrow."

I pulled her off the tailgate, held her tight and pecked her cheek and said "Goodnight."

I walked her back to the front door and said goodnight again, then turned and walked back to my truck. On my way out, I looked through the window next to the front door and saw her watching me as I rolled out slowly.

"Thank you, Lord, for tonight," I prayed.

Whatever I had done, I had done it right. I didn't really try, but I had said or done something right. She had said or done something too, something that made me want her more than I already had. I had never fallen so fast for anyone in my life, and I would try to put on the breaks as much as possible. I knew though no matter how hard I tried; nature would take its course. Like a bird soaring through the heavens, I was free. And like a boulder rolling down a hill, she was falling faster and faster for me, as if she was playing catch-up for all the years lost. We had both been through our share of hardships—just two ordinary people put in extraordinary situations who ended up finding each other; an undying flame, possessed by two hearts that nothing could ever put out; two souls looking for love on the same pedestrian-packed sidewalks of life and happened to bump shoulders.

I drove home slow wanting to savor the magic. It would be tough for me to go to sleep tonight. I started to think about what I was going to do tomorrow. It would be my last day to see her; the next day I would be gone halfway around the world. Then I decided, *Hey, I'm a moment man, I live in the moment.* One minute at a time, nothing is scheduled, nothing is planned. Plans are only markers for failure. You can plan only so much then comes reality—cold cruel realism. Now I do have goals, which are different. A goal is something you hope to accomplish, a plan is something you want and intend on happening. So I decided to allow whatever happened to happen, maybe we would kiss; maybe the moment wouldn't be right.

She had been unable to sleep too, not because of Tyson—no, he slept sound tonight. Her mind ran rampant with thoughts of how and why she had allowed herself to fall that fast. She thought, *I've never felt like this. Could this be love? Is this what real love was? It couldn't be; he'd practically been a stranger, a figment for all these years. It's almost like he just popped up, and bam! I feel like this now. You can't fall in love this fast. Oh, but what if you can? Even if I am, I have to hold out longer than this. I have to know that he feels the same way. Well, of course he does. But what if he doesn't? Oh, I'll give him a chance. What am I talking about? If he didn't really care, he would have kissed me tonight.* She finally ended up on *he does care, and I'll give him a chance.*

I got home around 1:00, walked to my room, and sat at the foot of my bed, contemplating on calling her. I wanted her to know how much I cared about her then decided me telling her that would do nothing; she would have to realize it on her own. I lay down, and like a waterfall sleep fell upon me. Once again I was awakened, by my little brother, in a cold sweat screaming. He asked me, "What were you screaming 'Get back, get back!' for?"

I looked at him with fear-struck eyes, still dazed, and said, "I don't remember. Was I really yelling that loud?"

"Yea, you know I can sleep through a train. You tried to hit me when I woke you up."

I laughed and said, "Sorry. Did I say anything else?"

"Yea, you said, 'Stay down, everyone stay down. Get the hell down.'"

"Wow, let's talk about something different. That's kind of freakin' me out."

"Okay, but I wanna know something real quick. Did you see a lot of action while you were there?"

Disgusted, I said, "Josh, I don't want to talk about it, okay. Does that answer your question?"

"I guess I just think it would be cool to be a marine and go to war."

I looked sternly disappointed at him then said, "There is nothing cool about war. There is nothing cool about people dying. Stuff happens that no man should have to see, no man should have to do. We are done talking about this until I'm ready. Do you understand?"

"Yea, yea, I'm sorry. They're talking about playing me on varsity next year. Outside linebacker."

"Oh yea, that's good. You could have played varsity this year, honestly. It's just politics. Dad doesn't go talk and hang out with the coaches like the other dads do."

"Yea, I guess that has something to do with it. So how was your date tonight?"

I smiled and left it at that.

He then asked, "You had sex with her, no way?"

I laughed and said, "No, Josh, I did not have sex with her, I care about her too much, and you know that. Besides, there's more to women than just sex, believe it or not. You'll learn that after a while. Nothing can ruin a relationship faster than sex. It makes people think too much, then they start assuming stuff, then there you are, single again. I didn't even kiss her."

"You don't really think all that, do you? I mean that and getting drunk is all you used to be about."

I smiled. I was a changed man.

"Well, about her I do, and one thing Iraq did do for me was put things in perspective, a new light. It made me appreciate all the little things that no one notices.

Do you ever imagine what it would be like to have no legs, or one finger, or a burned face? Probably not, unless you're walking down the street and see someone with those problems. It changed my appreciation for life."

"Yea, I thought I noticed something different, it's good, I guess. I still wanna party though."

I laughed then said, "Well, do it, party it up. I'm not gonna stop you, just be smart about it, and someday you'll look back through different eyes and see all the other things you could have done. Hind sights 20/20 right."

"Yea. Hey I'm gonna go back to bed, I got school in like three hours."

"Okay, sleep well and keep those grades up. Love you, Josh."

"Love you too, Adam, 'night."

I wondered what I was dreaming earlier, but then again did I really want to know? It wasn't a flashback. I was never in that situation in Iraq; I had never said that. I decided to stop thinking about it. I couldn't go back to sleep. Even though I was tired, I didn't really want to. I walked outside to the back porch I'd helped my dad build. Well, he did most of the work; I actually played a very minimal part in its construction. The rain had brought in a cool front. It felt nice out. The stars were still bright out the clouds had passed. My dog Zeke, a Siberian husky part Rottweiler, ran his head up between my arm and the chair I had picked to sit in. He softly moaned wanting some attention. I reached up and put my hand on his head then began petting.

I said, "Hey there, boy. I had a great night tonight. Leslie is an amazing girl." He softly growled, and I replied, "Yea, you'll get to see her tomorrow. She'll like you a lot. Hey boy, I'm tired; I'm gonna go get some sleep now. I'll see you tomorrow."

I patted him and went back inside and fell asleep on the couch.

I woke up around 9:30. I had a missed text message from Leslie.

It said, "Hey I had a great time last night, you are an amazing man, can't wait to see you."

FAREWELL

DON'T BE A STRANGER

TODAY WAS A murky day; the clouds were low and hazy. The pond in the front pasture lay still and stagnant. Our horses lay out in the field rolling around in the mud and muck. They were enjoying the day, at least. The air had warmed back up, and due to the rain the night before, it was extremely humid—not the greatest of conditions to share with a woman.

I couldn't stop thinking about last night. When people say dreams come true, well, it's true. Since the first day I laid eyes on her, I'd wanted her. It started out as lust simply because she was just so beautiful. Then getting to know her especially last night, I saw what real, true, genuine beauty was. I wanted to kiss her tonight but at the same time not rush it. If I kissed her, I would have something to go back with. If I didn't, well then, I would want to even more, and I hoped she would feel the same. It was definitely going to be a long day; I was bored and needed to free my mind before I drove myself crazy. I walked out to the barn, remembering my dad had asked me to give the horses some dry hay. We had three of them, a filly, a mare, and gelding. All were purebred quarter horses. Normally, if they weren't so muddy, they were beautiful. After I had completed that task, I walked over to the makeshift dock I always liked to leave my worries and concerns at. There were a few water moccasins skating across the pond, so I grabbed the shotgun and some ammo. I rocked to and fro in the same rusted iron rocking chair as I had before, waiting and waiting for them to get in range. Then they did...

With the pull of the trigger, my mind's eye traveled back to the deployment.

Bam!

"Crap, take cover, *sniper*!" our squad leader yelled.

I took off to the left, my buddy Jesse took off to the right. I baseball slid behind a glass phone booth until I realized they can still get me here. I picked myself up and ran about ten meters to the side of a building. Jesse, meanwhile, had separated himself from the squad on the other side of the road behind a concrete roadblock.

I yelled, "Jess, you okay?" as a three-round burst smacked right above his head.

He yelled, "Shoot! Green, cover me, I'm coming over!"

Before I could say, "What do you want me to cover? I don't know where he is!" he had hurdled the barrier and was in a viciously fast sprint to my building. Then *snap, snap, snap,* three more rounds were laid out in front of one foot, then in between, then right behind. I popped around the corner and shot at the nearest building that looked like it might be a sniper position. I got off twelve rounds from my M16 before he got over there with me. When he got close, he ducked his shoulder and tackled me back behind the cover of the wall and rolled across me, landing on his feet majestically.

I yelled at him, "What the heck was that for!"

He replied in an adrenaline rush full of sarcasm, "I saw where he was on the way, and you weren't shooting anywhere near him."

Then he said, "Look at that wall," pointing right behind where I had popped out. There was a hole in it right at my level; a round would have hit me if he didn't tackle me.

Then he said, "Hey, when you popped around the corner, did you see that house with all the graffiti on it?"

"Yea, man, I saw it."

"Okay. The top left window I saw muzzle flashes; it's the window with the glass in a widow's peak. On three, I'm gonna pop around the corner and start poppin' at it. You run around and post up behind that boulder right there."

"Okay, on three. When I get there, I'll suppress, you move up, then I'll run up and charge through the door."

Then I thought, *Wait, there might be a booby trap on the door*, and said, "No, I'm gonna dive through the window; you better be right on me."

Both our nerves were on edge as he counted down. "Three, two, one." *Pop, pop, pop,* he started shooting, and I button hooked around him, ran and knelt down behind the rock. I picked up the fire on the window, shooting as accurately as my shaky hands would allow. He ran up to the house and stood tactically against the wall. The sniper then turned his attention to me as he shot of a burst directly to the right of the rock I was behind.

I ducked behind it, taking cover and yelled, "Frag it, frag it!"

He pulled the pin, popped the spoon, then let it fly through the window; as soon as it went off, I was in a rush straight to the window. As I dived, I held my muzzle above my kevlar, making sure the muzzle would hit the glass before I did and went straight through. I rolled and popped right up, I turned around, and Jesse was already there inside with me. He took off for the stairs. As soon as he got in, I fell in at number 2 man. He got to the top and covered the window; he whispered, "second room, right side." I tactically walked to the edge of the doorway as he stacked behind me.

I gave the countdown to charge the room, "Three, Two..."

Before I could get to one, a grenade slowly rolled out into the hallway about a foot from me. Instinct kicked in and I booted it back in the room then turned and dived into Jesse, knocking him down, getting both of us out of the way of the potential blast. As soon as this one blew, I charged the room to see two insurgents lying on the ground, all bloody from the shrapnel that pierced their bodies. One lay facedown, the other lay face up, bleeding out of his skull, throat, and chest as he took his last few breaths, on his way to meet the marines that guard heaven's gates. *Good luck getting in, punk.* I went over to the other to do a dead check. I rammed my muzzle into his ribs. He didn't move. We began to flip the room inside out.

I turn around to see Jesse put two rounds in the guy I'd just dead checked as he yelled, "Grenade! Get down!"

I hit the deck like a rock. The insurgent had rolled over just a little bit, revealing a grenade he'd just pulled. I stood up after the blast, which had gone off less than five feet away from me; I was untouched. The insurgent's body had shielded me from everything except blood and gore. I called over the radio for two body bags and told them the sniper threat had been eliminated. Snap back to reality.

I missed the snakes; they swam into the tall grass at the bank and weren't seen again. There's nothing quite like a flashback; you remember the drastic details but not the things you wished you would remember. There were a few good things we did, a few good times we had. If you asked me, though, it would take me a while to remember, if I could even remember. I sat there for about an hour more, building a sweat before I went back into the house. I went to my room and dug a letter out of my seabag that I had wrote to Leslie while I'd been in Iraq. I read over it.

Dear Leslie,

How are you doing? I heard you just had your baby? What's his name? Well, I just wanted to tell you congratulations.

It's pretty rough over here, nothing like I'd expected though. How's your family doing? When's the next time your dad comes home? I don't really know how to say this, so I'm just gonna give it a shot.

I know we haven't exactly spent the most time together, and I know you probably don't even think about me. I have had a crush on you for a long time, and I would love to tell you in person, but I may not get that opportunity. I just wanted you to know that. I know you don't see me the same way, but I would like to get the chance to show you who I am. Then maybe you could look at me differently. So if you don't mind, when I come home, going to a movie or doing something with me. You know, just so we can talk for a little while. There's so much I want to tell you, but I don't know how to write it. I don't expect you to write me back or feel the same way I do. I'm practically a stranger I know. That's why I'm asking for a chance to not be. You are a beautiful young woman both inside and out, and I'm sure your son is too... only not the woman part. Hopefully he takes after his momma. I don't want to end this letter on a weird note, so here's a joke; hopefully you'll think it's as dumb as I do and laugh. How were the great lakes formed? Chuck Norris was bored and went for a walk. Here's another one.

> Chuck Norris's tears can cure cancer; it's too bad he never cries. That's all I got, hopefully you enjoyed them. I really hope to see you when I get back, thanks for reading.
>
> Sincerely,
> Adam

I was glad I never sent this one; I didn't think it would have had the same effect. It was one of the few that I had actually kept. I'd written so many and only one seemed to say what I wanted to say. Even then, the words couldn't truly explain the way I thought.

I walked around the house, vacuumed, and took the trash out. How would tonight go? What would she think? I had never brought a girl home with my family there. It made me even more nervous. Could I, even if the moment was right, talk how I wanted to, or kiss her? A million questions plagued my mind. She should be coming over any minute now, so I hopped in the shower.

I was excited as she pulled up. I sat there on the front porch, with Zeke keeping me company. I walked down and out to the car when she parked; Tyson was in the backseat asleep. I wondered how babies could sleep in the most awkward positions. He had his legs crossed, both hands lying to the left and his head to the right with a pacifier in his mouth. She was always beautiful. She was wearing a white T-shirt and orange shorts.

I said nervously, "How was your day? You look good."

She smiled and said, "You're a dork. My day was good, and thanks. What have you done all day?"

"Why am I a dork?"

She laughed then said as she hugged me, "I don't know; it's not a bad kind of dork."

"Oh, I didn't realize there were certain kinds of dorks."

"Well, it's just I can tell you're nervous, and I don't know why. You weren't that nervous last night."

"Yea, I was. You're smokin' hot, and, well, I'm…I'm just me. I'll try to not be shy okay? I had a great time last night too. Oh, I got your text earlier today."

She laughed then said, "You're a good dork, so can we come in, or are you just gonna make me stand out here all day?"

I smiled and said, "Well, I'd thought about it; I guess if you really wanna come in, you can."

She grabbed Tyson, and we walked up the stairs to the house. I wanted to hold her free hand but settled for just brushing it.

I opened the door then said, "You want me to show you around?"

"Sure, let me put Tyson down while he's still sleeping. I swear he sleeps at the weirdest times."

I laughed and said, "Well, he does it on purpose, you know. He says 'I'm gonna make Momma get up in the middle of the night.'"

"Sometimes I think so."

I showed her around the house, then we decided to settle for the living room. We talked and rolled around with Tyson, and when my parents got home we all had dinner together.

After dinner I asked, "Leslie, you wanna go for a walk or go sit out on the dock?"

"I'd like that. Let me make Tyson a bottle real quick."

We walked outside as the sun began to fade on its way to becoming part of the earth. The ground was slightly wet because of a little shower while we'd been inside. The old burned tree hung over the dock providing a picture-perfect silhouette. The wind was smooth, coming in slow waves. As we sat there, we didn't talk much; just stared at each other or enjoyed the pinks and oranges of God's paintbrush in the sky. The cows mooed in the background providing a nice redneck romance. As we sat down at the dock, I looked over at her holding Tyson, waved at him, looked back at her, and started laughing.

She laughed a nervous laugh and said, "What's so funny? What are you laughing for?"

I smiled as I said, "It's just that I have always dreamed of this; now that it's here, I don't know what to say or do. You are so beautiful, and I have wanted to be with you for so long. Leslie, I have never liked anyone as much as I like you."

She smiled a tearful smile and said, "You must have a lot of nightmares then. I mean, you can't really feel like that. I have a kid that's not yours. I've never slept with you; hell, I've never even kissed you. You can't feel like that."

I was kind of shocked by this little episode, but at the same time it was a topic that would have to be talked about eventually.

Better sooner than later, I thought as I smiled and said, "Well, there are some things in life that mean more than sex and making out; to me you do. I don't care about Tyson, I mean, I do care about him, but whether or not he's mine, that doesn't change the way I feel about you, or about him."

I leaned over and gave her a kiss on the cheek and rubbed Tyson's little head. She looked compelled as if she'd never heard something like that or never expected to hear something like that.

Then I said, "It's really a beautiful evening tonight. You know why I started watching sunsets?"

She smiled and said, "You are so sweet. What is it about you? You're different than other guys. I mean, really, you're different. How can you really feel like that?"

"Well, as for being different, I'm just me; what you see is what you get. I'm nothing special, and I know that. I believe that everything happens for a reason, who am I to argue with God? I don't follow the crowd anymore; look where it got me, in the Marine Corps 3,000 miles away from my family. And as for me feeling like that, well, I guess when you want something bad enough, you just gotta have it regardless the circumstances... While I was in Iraq, I was set up in a blocking position next to the Euphrates river right before the sun came up. It reminded me of back home. It put me at peace for a second, and I told myself when I get back I'm gonna watch more sunrises and sunsets. It gave me appreciation for natural beauty. I thought of you, I thought of the dance at prom. So now, I look at the sun in its most majestic raw state and think of you." While I'd been talking, she had slid her hand over and intertwined her fingers with mine.

She smiled with a tear in her eye and said, "I've never heard something like that before. I've never felt like this before. I keep saying that, but you keep saying things like that, and it's just like, well, I don't know... that different thing about you; I like it. I like you...I have to be going, though, I have to go to a wedding rehearsal tomorrow pretty early."

I was disappointed, but I felt like tonight went well. I had to wake up early as well to catch my flight back.

I smiled and said, "Well, Leslie, I have had a great time the last few days. I hate that I have to leave tomorrow. Don't be a stranger."

She laughed and said, "What, do you think just because you're leaving, I'm not gonna talk to you? I had a great time too. What time is your flight?" We got up as the sun lowered past the horizon blue and gold streaked the sky. We began the slow walk to the car.

I smiled, wanting to hold her hand but restrained myself and said, "It's at 10:30, but we have to leave the house at 6 to get there on time. I'll call you when I land?"

"Well, you better call me."

She put Tyson in the car seat, then we stood there next to the car for a minute holding each other.

Then I said, "I'm gonna miss you. Drive safe and have fun at the wedding."

"I'm gonna miss you too. You have fun shooting guns and stuff. Good-bye, Adam."

"Good-bye." I said and closed her door.

I turned and walked up the steps as she rolled away like a thief in the dark with my heart. Like an old shirt, I'd been pulled out of the drawer. As hard as it was to start talking to her, it was even tougher to watch her leave. The night wind whispered notes of love. I knew how she felt, and she knew how I felt. The feelings were mutual; I had brought her feelings to even playing field practically overnight. I was glad I didn't kiss her, as right as it felt to; it felt like if I waited, it would be better. I thanked God for the flame he'd placed in my life. The stars were out tonight, the hazy clouds had parted. The night had ended perfect; I couldn't ask for a better ending. There it was at the tip of my fingers, the whole world at my hands. She had suddenly become more than a friend; she had become more than I had ever thought—she had become my world.

BLOSSOMING AWAY

THE FLIGHT BACK was rough. I'd never really had a problem before. Normally, I'd be home for more than five days and be ready to go back to work. This time though, I'd found something worth staying for, minus of course all the legal trouble I'd get in if I did stay. As much as I wanted to stay and just hold her tight in my arms, I couldn't. It was an eight-hour flight halfway across the world.

Leslie and I talked extensively over the next week. I congratulated her on graduating, and she congratulated me on getting our new marines. We talked about life and favorite colors, just picking each other apart for any little bit of information we could think of. I told my roommates about the time I'd had with her.

Then Mike said, "Well, are ya'll goin out yet?"

"Well, yea, I think so. I haven't really asked her, but the way we talk, I'd say yea."

He looked at me with disappointment and grabbed me by the shoulder then said, "If you haven't asked, it's not official. You have to ask; that way if something happens, she can't say, 'We weren't even going out.' You know what I'm saying? Haven't I taught you anything? Ah."

"Yea, so next time I talk to her, I should ask her to be my girlfriend?"

"Well, if it feels like the right moment."

This was great advice. When the heck was the right moment? Leslie and I talked a lot every day since I'd been gone; a few hours at least every day.

Her favorite color was green; she said it made her hair look good. She always looked good though. She hated her job; she said she had a stalker there named Tanner. She said he always tried to talk to her, and she was just disgusted by his presence. I told her about my stalker, a girl I'd dated for a week in the eighth grade who still somehow would manage to find out where I was. We talked about each other, complementing anything and everything we could. She asked what my take on sex and love is.

I answered honestly, saying, "Love is a feeling shared by two people. It is the thing that makes people special to each other. It has nothing to do with sex. Sex is the act of showing love, but at the same time there are so many other ways to show you love someone."

Then she said, "That's a good definition. Are you a virgin?"

I sighed and said, "No, unfortunately."

"Yes, you are; you're just trying to brag."

I wasn't joking, so I said, "No, I really am not. I regret it, because quite frankly it wasn't worth it." Now I had never been hurt due to sex but had seen people who had, and the numbers for hurt were greater than those not.

She said laughing, "Oh, I always saw you as this innocent little boy."

I replied, "Thus Tyson, how many people?"

"You first; I'm a lady, that's not polite to ask?"

"Oh, well in that case, I've been with three, had sex with one girlfriend, the rest were one-night stands. I lost my virginity when I was eighteen in a movie theater. I have never loved anyone before. I've had eight girlfriends, none very long, because I have a huge problem with commitment. Now, it's your turn, sweetie, spill the beans."

Now I could have probably left out the part about commitment, but I said it. I wanted to be completely honest with her as if I had nothing worth hiding.

She said quietly "Wow, you're a bad boy, I never saw you like that."

Then I said, "What good is it to lie to you? It does me no good."

With confidence and trust in her voice, she said, "You're right; I've had sex with three guys. I lost my virginity in the back of a truck when I was fifteen to a guy I thought loved me, and I thought I loved him. He treated me like crap, and I thought that's what love was. In fact, all my past boyfriends have treated me like crap. I've never had a one-night stand."

This was the moment, I decided. Of all the times I could have picked, I picked right after the sex talk.

"Leslie, I like you a lot. I will never lie to you, and I will never treat you like you've been treated, I promise this. I'm not very good at this. I've never done this over the phone before. Um, will you be my girlfriend?"

As she laughed, she said, "Of course, I will. I was starting to worry you wouldn't ask me. You're right; you're not very good at that. I know you won't treat me like that."

I said like an idiot, "Really? Cause you don't have to if you don't want."

"Adam, just shut up, you're a dork. I want to go out with you."

I had done it—dream number 2; I was officially dating Leslie Ranor. The date was May 27th.

It was a five-hour time difference from me to her. She talked to me every night from around 11:00 to later than midnight, her time. Then I would wake up at 4:30 to talk to her from then until 5:30 when I had to go run. Then there would be random calls on and off all day.

The next talk we had, I said after we'd been talking for a little while, "I hate to ask this, but I think I need to. Are you sure you can handle a long-distance relationship? I mean, the next time I'll be home is December. Then after that, I go back to Iraq, and we probably won't get to talk that much."

I didn't want to talk about that, not after how far we'd come. The thing was I needed to know before I let my emotions go.

She replied, "Of course I can handle it. I have never felt like this about anyone. When you're in Iraq, we can write. I can do it, I promise." She said this with such sincerity, such conviction, I believed her. I knew it would be tough, but I also knew her and the way she felt, and it was real.

I had to go to the rifle range this week to re-qualify on my M16 and get qualified on the M9 pistol. I wouldn't be able to talk to her as much as I wanted.

She said, "It's okay, sweetie. Can I still text you?"

"Yes, ma'am, you may, and we should be getting off earlier than 1700 every day, sorry, 5:00 I mean, so I should be able to call you after I'm done shooting, but I can text you in between rotations."

She laughed and said, "You're a dork, so how are you gonna shoot?"

I smiled then said, "Well, you know me, I'm straight gangsta yo, I'm gonna get expert fo sho. I can't be a dork, I'm too gangsta, sweetie."

"Okay, you're a gangster, my gangster. Have I ever told you you're amazing?" She paused then squealed, "Oh, I can't wait till December when I get to see you and finally kiss your face. I'm so excited."

"Well, have I ever told you I have the greatest girlfriend in the world? And if you want, you can come out here and see me; I really want to see you."

"I really want to see you, too, and hold your hand, but how am I gonna get out there? You know I don't make enough money for that, and how would Tyson get out there?"

"Well, we have five days off for the 4th of July, and I was thinking I'd fly you and Tyson out here, that's if you want to?"

"It's not that I don't, it's just that…I would feel bad taking your money."

"Leslie, you're not taking my money. Look at it this way. I want to see you, you want to see me, and this is a gift for both of us. Just think about it. I don't want an answer right now, just think about it."

"You are so sweet; did you want to kiss me before you left?"

I smiled a sad smile, already missing her memory. "Leslie, you have no idea. It would have been a dream come true, but everything happens for a reason, and I didn't want to ruin anything. I mean, who's to say if I did kiss you we would be where we are today? I like where we are today. Besides, I'm not into the whole kissing on the first date."

I could tell she was smiling halfway across the world as she said, "Oh, so I guess it was a date, huh? I'm just kidding. I really wanted to kiss you too. When you were changing the tire, when you left my house that night, and when I left your house. Oh, I can't wait to finally be able to kiss my boyfriend and hold your hand."

I was feeling kind of daring now, so I said, "What are you wearing right now?"

She laughed and said, "Wouldn't you like to know?"

I laughed and said, "Yea, I wanna image of my girlfriend, seeing as I don't have a picture to look at."

She said in a seductive tone "Well, I'm wearing a yellow Eagles shirt, and it's getting kind of hot in my room right now."

"Oh, really, someone's talkin dirty. You wanna know what I'm wearing?"

"I am not talkin dirty. I always sleep naked, it feels better. Underwear gives me a wedgie and thongs are uncomfortable. What are you wearing?"

"Well, since we're not talkin' dirty right now, I'm not gonna tell you that I'm wearing my uniform. You know my charlies(Green dress uniform the marines have), the ones I wore to church while I was home."

I wasn't, but I knew how much she liked it.

"You looked so good that day. I wanted to kiss you right there, but I don't know if that would have been appropriate for church. You know I love a man in uniform, especially a hot, bald one. Ha ha ha."

She sounded tired, and it was getting late. I had to wake up early at 0300 to catch the bus out to the rifle range. I knew when she was tired, I knew her moods; she never really got moody, though. We had been dating officially for about two weeks now; we never argued. I don't know if this was a good or bad thing. I was still nervous talking to her, but slowly, ever so slowly, she was breaking me out of my shell. I was falling in love—I was in love. It was weird; I'd never felt like this before, an emotion I had no experience in. Normally, I had something to complain about. Work was getting more ridiculous by the day. But I never found myself in a bad mood, because just as I started feeling blue, she would call or text me, automatically bringing my spirits back up. Life was wonderful. She was wonderful.

We talked much more than I thought we would be able to that week. I think it was simply because I put her before work. She meant more to me than work. It was Wednesday night, June 13th. She called, and we talked for a while about each other's days and a few random topics.

Then I said, "Let's play the question game, I ask a question, then you ask one."

"Okay, I'll start. How did you shoot today?"

"Well, I was hoping you wouldn't ask. I guess I'm not quite as gangsta as I thought. I shot sharpshooter, which is the middle award."

"Oh, I'm sorry. I wasn't distracting you, was I?"

I smiled and said, "Yea, but it was a good distraction. I wouldn't trade my score for talking to you."

"I'm sorry, your still gangster to me, you dork. It's your turn now."

I wanted the conversation to move fast. I wanted it to move to more deep, more compelling things.

So I asked, "Okay, what did I do to get you? I mean, I never did anything too special. I'm not a special guy, and I still can't see what I did."

She paused for a minute, gathering her emotions, then said, "I guess I never really knew who you were until I got your letter. Then when we went out that night, I knew there was something different about you, something sweet and innocent. You don't care what I've done, you just make me feel special. You make me feel different. I like the way you make me feel. Every day, you know just what to say to make me feel better. So what made you fall for me?"

I didn't really see what she was trying to say, but it was sweet. I was always just me; I never strayed to impress her. I guess we were just a perfect couple, a match made in heaven.

I said in response, "Like I wrote in the letter, ever since the first day I saw you, I knew...You are beautiful both inside and out, I guess that's where you got me. Now then, my turn huh. What do you see different in me than all your past boyfriends?"

I could hear her smile as she said, "There's a lot of things. First, you don't try to buy me, which is what the last one did. And you are mature. You're very smart; I learn something pointless every time I talk to you, ha ha ha. I mean, you know a lot of useless stuff, and I think it's cute. The main thing is I have never had anyone treat me like you do. I have told you things I haven't even told my mother."

We went back and forth a few more questions before I was able to say what I really wanted to say, and that was "I love you." I knew it was soon, but I just couldn't hold it. I had made it this far on fifty-fifty chances. What would one more hurt? The letter was a hit or miss. The first date was a hit or miss. The same when I asked her out. I wanted to say it, but I didn't want to hear it if she didn't mean it.

So I said, "Would you be freaked out if I told you how I really feel about you, if I told you that I loved you?"

She said in an I-want-to-hear-it voice, "No."

"I do, Leslie. I love you, but I don't want you to say it back if you don't really mean it. I won't say it anymore until you're ready, because I don't want to pressure you into anything. You mean too much to me."

That was it, I was done. I'd swung and struck out. I knew she didn't feel the same yet, she was close, but with everything she'd been through, I knew she would put her guard up.

She said, "You are so sweet, and I like you a lot, but I don't know if I love you yet; I mean, we haven't even been dating but like three weeks if that. Don't be sorry, I could tell you wanted to get that off your chest, and I really wanted to hear it. Thank you for being so respectful."

That was a better answer than I'd expected. We talked a little while longer, slowly easing the conversation down. Then we got off. I lay down in my cot using my extra pants as a pillow and stared at the ceiling for a while.

Then I got a text message saying, "You are an amazing man, and you make me feel like no one can. I don't know what it is, but I keep falling faster for you. Whatever it is keep it up, 'cause I love it, and I can't wait to kiss you. You're my little gangster."

I began to do something I hadn't done in quite a while, I dreamed. I dreamed peaceful. I hadn't really slept well since we got back. The room was loud; there were about thirty of us in there. We had to stay in a squad bay for the week. I chose a cot to sleep on instead of a mattress, because I thought I slept better on them. I only slept about four hours, but it was the best four hours of sleep a man could ask for. I knew it wouldn't be long before she said those three little words that mean so much. Now it was just a matter of time. We had a little bit more firing to do tomorrow, and then the next day we would go back to base.

I talked to Leslie every day the following week. I made jokes; she called me a dork and would laugh. We talked about life, religion, and right and wrong. Our opinions were pretty much the same, just with small variations. Anything and everything we could talk about we did, and when there was nothing left to talk about, we listened to each other's wildly beating hearts. She would talk dirty jokingly, then I would talk dirty seriously. I could hear her breaths getting shorter by the second, a moan every now and then. Then I would stop, slowly but steadily teasing her over the phone.

I asked her that Wednesday after talking for a while, "So, Leslie Ranor, I was just wondering if you'd considered my offer?"

"What offer?"

I laughed and said, "To be my rap partner. You know you can keep the beat, and I can do my thing. No, would you like to come out here and visit me? I really want to see you."

She laughed and said, "You're a dork. Yes, I thought about it and I'm terrified of flying, I've never flown before, but I really want to see you, too, so yes, but I need a car seat for Tyson."

I smiled and said, "You have no idea how happy I am right now, but can't you just hold Tyson..."

She started to speak before I cut her off saying, "Of course, I'll get Tyson a car seat. My staff sergeant has kids; I'm sure he'll let me borrow one. Does the 5th through the 10th sound good?"

"That sounds awesome, but can I stay any longer?"

I was taken aback by that; I figured five days would be good enough.

I said, "Well, how long did you want to stay? I mean, I really only have those days off. Other than that, I'm gonna have to work from 0600 to 1700."

In a loving voice, she said, "Well, I was hoping I could stay with you forever. Ha ha ha. No, five days is good, I guess."

Even if she was joking, that was a sign of something more, something great. I'd never talked to girls like this before. Most of the time we would talk, then she would keep calling; I would get annoyed then I would break it off. She was different, she was exciting. She kept me intrigued.

It was Saturday, June 23; so far, the day had been pretty crappy for me. We had had to work that morning. It was only four hours, but it took away from our Friday night and Saturday morning. I also had a machine gun section BBQ, which quite frankly I didn't want to go to. It was overcast outside, and I hadn't heard from Leslie since 5 that morning. She had to work today. She hated her job, which she'd been working at for about a year now. She said she'd been trying to find a job for a while, but either they didn't pay enough to support her and her son, or they wouldn't take on the challenge of hiring a teenage mother. There were definitely a lot of obstacles she had to face in her position. From my opinion, she was hurdling them one by one, and slowly but surely she was moving forward with the world against her. I never told her she couldn't do it or even hinted toward it, because deep inside I knew she could. It would be extremely tough, but with her strong-willed determination, I knew she could do it. I wanted to be the one to help. She didn't need it, of course, but a free hand is always good. As long as she kept to the path she was on, she would succeed.

I went over to the BBQ at my staff sergeant's house. On my way there, I called Leslie. I knew she was still at work so I just left a message.

"Hey, sweetie, hope your day was great and you got a lot of tips. I'm gonna be busy for the next few hours. I have that BBQ I promised I'd go to, but, hey, it's free food right. Well, can't wait to talk to you. You can text me if you want; otherwise, I'll call you when I'm done over here. Bye-bye."

I wanted to say I love you so bad, but I told her I wouldn't until she was ready, and I am a man of my word, so I didn't.

❧

We got there, and SSgt. Slate asked, "Who likes to cook? I need some help with the grill."

I was trying to stay under the radar until my buddies said, "Green! He's freakin' awesome. Take Green, staff sergeant."

Before I could deny it, he said, "Good. Green, get over here. You want a beer? Someone get this man a beer."

"No, staff sergeant, I quit drinkin'. Besides, I'm Tompson's designated driver."

He replied, "Okay, good on you. I guess you decided to quit throwin' limes at people from hotels."

I laughed along with everyone else at his wisecrack then said, "Yes, staff sergeant, I switched to paper airplanes, they don't hurt as bad from twenty-two stories up." They all got a laugh out of that. The year before, before I went to Iraq, I'd had a little incident.

My buddy Mike and I had got a hotel room on the twenty-second deck and were throwing a party. We had been drinking all day since 9:00 that morning. Everyone showed up then left, and right before they came back, we got the bright idea to throw empty beer bottles out in the intersection below. The streets were vacant because it was almost midnight now, so we just hurled a few, seeing who could throw farther. He won.

Then some local people were walking on the sidewalk and I, in all my drunken wisdom, say, "Hey, I bet I can hit that guy with a lime."

To which Mike replied, "Dude, no way. There is no way your drunk, uncoordinated butt can hit 'im. You could barely even get the intersection." Well, I took that as a challenge and took a running step and let it fly.

About five seconds later, we heard a guy screaming like bloody murder, and his buddy say, "Was that a freakin' lime?"

Now if we'd have been smart, we would have gotten in the room and turned off the lights, but in our drunken stupor, we decided to point and laugh. Everyone showed back up, about twelve guys other than us. Mike went to go piss. Not even five minutes after everyone got back, we hear a knock at the door. Mike, being the closest to it, answers. It was the police. They cuffed him as I chugged my last beer and then kicked us out. I ran after the cop car all the way to the police station and tried to bail him out.

They said, "Sir, we know you've been drinking; underage too. We're gonna have to arrest you, too, if you don't leave right now."

I was prepared to go down with my friend, so I yelled back, slurring my words into the holding cell. "Hey, Mike, I'm gonna get you out. What do you want me to do?"

Without any hesitation, he yelled back, "Go away, I'll see you tomorrow."

"Okay. Later, man."

I went to the top and waited for him to get military escorted back to base. We both got in trouble for that. I got put on restriction and extra duties and had to fork over a bunch of money. He got the same plus his rank taken away. His punishment was more severe because he was the one that got arrested. On top of that, we both had to attend AA meetings and a few alcohol awareness classes. We had both been getting picked on for it for over a year. We had become infamous throughout the battalion. They mentioned us, or at least the incident, in most all of the liberty briefs. After the fact, I realized how stupid my actions were and what could have happened. I felt really bad about it and wished I knew who I hit so I could apologize.

Staff sergeant said, "After we're all done eating, we're gonna play some horseshoes. And Green, try not to hit the power line this time."

Everyone laughed. I had thrown a horseshoe last year at one of these BBQs and almost took out a power line.

I replied quickly saying, "Okay, I'm on staff sergeant's team; ha, I called it."

He hadn't expected me to be that quick and didn't even have a response. We ate as much as we could fit then went out for the game.

Before the game started, I got a text from Leslie saying "I'm off work now; I can't stop thinking about you. You are an amazing man, and I can't wait to see you. You make my world go 'round and I love it, I..."

This was not fair; she was teasing me, but I loved it. I knew what she was about to say, and I wanted to hear it. I almost needed to hear it.

I replied, "Hope you had a great day. I couldn't stop thinking about you too. You mean so much to me, Leslie, I just wanted you to know that."

I wanted to ask, "I...what?" but I decided not to. I had told her I wouldn't put any pressure on her, and I wouldn't. I couldn't let myself. My first throw of the horseshoes was almost a repeat of last year, only this time I was slightly distracted. Right before the next throw, I got the message.

It said, "Te amo."

Now I knew what that meant, but for confirmation I asked my Mexican buddy Eddie what it meant.

He said, "She loves you."

I said, "Thanks, that's what I thought."

I had finally heard it. My heart soared away along with the horseshoe. I wanted to hear it in English, though; I didn't want her to be embarrassed by it. I was kind of embarrassed when I said it without hearing it in a response.

I replied to it. "I don't speak Spanish. What's that mean?"

Suddenly, my day had turned around. I had gone from a less than ecstatic mood to high as a dove floating on the clouds.

I said, "Staff sergeant, I'm gonna have to take a rain check on the rest of the game. I know you're gonna miss me, but I have some stuff I have to take care of."

To which he replied, "Can I get someone to salvage the score?"

I walked over to the wooden bench under the carport and sat down, kicked my legs up, and relaxed. I thought about her and Tyson, and the time we'd spent rolling and playing around upstairs in her room. We'd been dating now for almost a month and hadn't even seen each other since we started. We were both living on phone calls and memories. It was tough but at the same time it was the greatest feeling ever—to know that you were developing together without each other. The next message I got was, "I love u, I feel like I always have. I never want this feeling to end. Call me when you leave."

You'd be surprised what those three little words can do to a man. It changed me; I wanted nothing but her. I would have to wait for about two more weeks before I could tell her in person. People throw love around like it's a lost puppy, but whenever that magical little word "love" is said in unison, is meant in unison, and is felt in unison, the boundaries for the extraordinary are endless. The possibilities are innumerable. Living words, undying words, that are more than just words, more than just feelings. Love is something more. It is a gift, the greatest gift anyone could give. I had experienced love before. My buddies had given their lives for mine, the greatest gift—the greatest sacrifice—all out of love.

I'd waited what seemed like an eternity to hear it. Like a ship at sea I was free; a mountain so high it parts through the clouds. I was on top of the world.

I replied, "I love you too, and I mean it from the bottom of my heart."

I sent it then waited about five minutes to call her.

I couldn't wipe the smile off my face as I said, "Hello, I'm calling for a beautiful young redhead."

She replied, "Well, sir, I think you've called the wrong place. It's just Leslie, can you settle for that?"

"Yes, ma'am, that's actually who I was callin' for. How was work today?"

She sighed and said, "It was miserable. First we weren't busy at all so it just drag on. And then Tanner started working there, and I had to train him. He scares me, but he said he knows you. He said y'all hung out a few times."

"Did he now? Because I don't know anyone named Tanner. Did he say how he knows me?"

"Yea, he said to ask you how you know him."

"Well, I don't know anyone by that name. He's hitting on you, you know that, right?"

"No, he's not; that's just disgusting."

I laughed at her innocence. "Yea, yea he is. That's how guys hit on girls who have boyfriends; they say they know him and they're homeboys or something. They say that as a conversation starter. Sorry babe, he's hittin' on you."

I laughed because I knew where her heart was, and it was nestled in my arms.

She said, "Eww, he grosses me out. He has a kid too, only he uses his son to get stuff, if you know what I mean. He parties all the time and, from what I've heard, plays women all the time; I hate guys like that. You're not gonna play me, are you?"

I laughed and said, "Of course not. I'm a gangsta not a playa. I'm sorry you had a bad day. Are you drivin' home right now?"

"Yea, and it's raining pretty bad, almost like the night of our first date. How was the BBQ?"

"Well, I'm still here; I just wanted to talk to you, but I can't now. I want you to drive safe. Talkin to me isn't too safe. You wanna call me when you get there?"

"Yea, I guess. I still wanna talk to you, though. Oh crap! Sorry about that, some car almost cut me off."

"That's why I'll talk to you when you get home okay."

"Okay."

I smiled and said, "Drive safe. I love you."

"Okay. I love you too."

I sat there, breathing in the smell of charcoal and cigarettes, and somehow I smelled her through it all, thinking how lucky I was. Our relationship was a story in itself unique to any other.

When she got home, she sent me a text saying, "I'm home. I'm gonna get a shower then feed and play with Tyson. I love you."

I text back. "So what are you gonna be wearing?" to which the response was simply "Nothing."

It was tough for me to think about her like that, I cared so much for her so most of the time I couldn't. I respected her too much. I just thought about her and the miracle that had landed me with her.

I'd only planned on staying about an hour and a half but ended up being there about four hours.

Mike said, "Free beer is worth staying for."

So I had to wait around for all the beer to disappear, or get pissed away. Staff sergeant had a fifty-year-old bottle of gentleman's Jack Daniels and insisted that everyone take a shot. Therefore, I ended up having to wait around another hour to get it out of my system. When I finally ended up getting back to the room, it was about 9:00, 2:00 Leslie's time. I called hoping I wouldn't wake her; I had planned on just leaving a message.

The phone rang, and in a groggy, tired voice Leslie answered, "Hello, sweetie, how was the BBQ?"

I smiled and replied, "I was hoping you wouldn't answer, you should be sleeping."

"Yea, it's okay. Tyson just woke up right before you called so I'm already awake."

I could hear him whining in the background.

"Well, tell him I said hi. How's my baby doing?"

"He's doing good, just bein' a pain in the butt now, aren't you? Yes you are."

"I was actually talking about you. Hey, have you heard the newest rumor floating around town?"

"Which one? There's so many."

"My little brother was telling me Brandon was saying the reason you broke up with him and got with me was because Tyson was mine. I thought that was amazing seeing as we've never had sex. I told him that's the best rumor I'd ever heard."

"No, I haven't heard that one, but it's a good one. Adam, what is it about you that makes me completely and totally in love? How can you love me like you do?"

I smiled. I didn't really have an answer so I just said, "Leslie, I don't know what it is, but I love you and

I do know that. As far as me, I'm just me; what you see is what you get. How the heck did you fall in love with me?"

She had gotten Tyson to go back to sleep now and was breathing hard as she said, "I feel like I've loved you my whole life. You're so sweet, and as innocent as you may not be, I still see it in you. You make me happy like no one else ever has, like no one else ever could. And I can't wait until I'm Mrs. Adam Green."

I felt the same way, but as fast as our relationship had been moving, I didn't want to be the first one to say it. When she said it, though, it struck me deep, like a penny smacking the ground after being dropped from the Empire State Building.

I said, "And Leslie Ranor, nothing would make me happier, but I have to wait for your dad to get back to ask him."

She moaned, "Oh, but why can't we just do it when I come out there?"

"I would love nothing more, but it wouldn't feel right if I didn't ask him. Sorry, I have no choice."

She said as she steadily breathed harder and harder until it turned into a seductive moan. "See, that's why I love you so much. You have so much respect. Oh, I can't wait till I finally get to kiss you and get my hands all over you. The first thing I'm gonna do when I get off that plane is kiss your face off."

"And I love you too. I'm gonna have a tough time controlling myself when you come down. I'm gonna hide from you in the airport, that way you think I forgot about you. I'm just kidding, I guess I'll give you a kiss. I think I'm gonna spend all day with you and Tyson then go back to my room at night so I don't do anything. Either that or I can sleep on the floor."

"You could do that, or you could stay with me and cuddle. I don't bite. But hey, I'm about to fall asleep on you. Can I get off now? I have to get ready for church early."

"No, you have to talk to me until it's time to wake up... I'm just kidding. Go to sleep, sweetie. I love you and I'll talk to you tomorrow."

"I love you too, goodnight."

I smiled. I knew those words would never get old. I walked outside to see everyone partying out on the catwalk.

"Green, have a beer with me," my buddy Lee said.

"Sorry man, I quit drinkin'."

"Since when, man? You know you used to be the drinkin' king."

"Yep, and now I'm relinquishing my crown to you. Congratulations."

I walked back in my room and wrote a poem. I was no poet; hell, I'd never even tried to write poetry before, but Leslie said she liked it so I thought I'd give it a shot.

DEVIL

I am in your first breath
I am your first tear of pain

I was your first friend but your worst enemy
I am the bully at school
I taught you your first curse word
I am the space between a fist and a face
I am the one who pulled them together
I am that feeling of doubt and pride
I breathed that first cigarette or joint
I tasted that first drop of alcohol
I am virginity lost
I made fun of you because you still are
I am the pulling force
I am the space between a bottle and your lips
I made you insecure
I am the reason for heartache
I am all the things in the world
I am always there for you
I am not wanted but persistent
I pulled the bullet to the heart
I am your best friend and worst enemy
I am your last breath
I am…

It was so tough to put my thoughts on paper, and when I finally did it, I just wasn't quite good enough. I read it to her anyway a few days later. She said it was the sweetest thing she'd ever heard. We talked about what to do when she came out here. We talked about how hard it was going to be to not have sex, and then we settled on, we would let it happen if it was the right moment. I wasn't planning on it. I wanted to, more than anything, but told myself I would not. She would be coming out the next day; I could hardly wait. My heart fluttered, my mind raced, and I knew everything would be all right. I had so much stuff planned for us to do. She said as long as she got to see me that was enough, but I wanted to make sure she would have plenty of memories. *Thank you, Lord,* I prayed, as I thought about all God had blessed me with. Not just for blessing me with her, but the simple things, like all my fingers and toes.

PASSION OF A LIFETIME

As I sat in the parking lot of the airport waiting, I pulled out my notepad and began to write another poem. She was so amazing, and as I waited my anticipation was soaring. I began to write.

MY LOVE

Leslie, my love
I love you, my love
Your face makes me smile
Your laugh makes me laugh
The love in your eyes burning into mine
I want to kiss your face
I want to hold you tight
I want to love you so
You amaze me
Your sweet words
The way you sound
The determination in your heart

The same heart I want to have
To hold and love and cherish
Will you love me, my love
As much as I love you?
I love you more than the sky has blue
Thank you, my love
Just for the dream you've made come true
I promise you, sweetheart, I'll do the same for you.

I had gone to the hotel earlier that day, setting up, trying my best to be as romantic as possible. I had it all planed out, but, of course, I knew how my plans usually ended up. So at the same time I planned, I canceled them out. Her flight just arrived; she would be in the baggage claim in about ten minutes. I walked inside and went up to the counter to buy a lei. I bought a yellow–and-green one, because they were her favorite colors. I was wearing a set of clothes my buddy Mike had picked out. He had a much better matching sense than I did. It was some red-colored Hawaiian board shorts and a marine corps green Hurley t-shirt. I had freshly shaved my head and sprayed some cologne on.

When she walked through the automatic doors leading into the baggage claim, I was stunned at her beauty. She carried Tyson on her hip with one arm. She was wearing a white tank top and orange pajama pants with a white stripe down the side. Her hair bounced. As she walked, her smile became immense as soon as she saw me. I walked toward her slowly; her magnificence left me almost idle. I pushed forward, though, and when we finally met, without saying a word, our mouths meshed—lips on lips, hearts in hearts, and love being expelled throughout our pores. The mob of people walked around us. Some stared, most just ignored us. Whatever the case, neither one of us cared. We had been waiting for this moment for a lifetime. She had anticipated the moment just as I had—both of us had fresh gum in our mouths.

I finally pulled away after what felt like forever and said, "You are truly beautiful, I love you."

I looked down at Tyson and gave him a kiss on the forehead as he rubbed his tired eyes, then said, "You too, buddy. How you doing?"

He looked up at me and smiled then turned his face and buried it in his mother's bosom.

She smiled at me, glimmering white teeth, eyes passionate, and said, "I have missed you so much, you don't even know. I can't wait till I can kiss you all over. I'm so excited."

With my continuing smile, I said, "Me too, I'm goin' straight for your back."

She giggled and said, "No, you can't do that. I'm not responsible for my actions if you do that; I will go crazy. I don't know if you can handle it."

"Oh, I know, I think I can handle it."

I kissed her again then stood there, watching the baggage wheel turn in circles, holding her hand. I could spend the rest of my life holding her hand. I could feel electric sparks of love running back and forth from her hand to mine. I grabbed her bags, and we set off for the hotel to drop off her luggage.

On the way there, the traffic was heavy, and she'd been awake for a long time. We talked for a while just catching up on the past few days.

I could see she was tired, so I told her, "You don't have to stay awake for me. Go to sleep, sweetie, and I'll wake you up when we get there."

She smiled and said, "Are you sure?"

"Yes. I'm a good driver; you got nothing to worry about."

"Okay."

Any time I was stopped at a light or in the thick of traffic, I found myself staring. She was truly a gift, a perfect mold from God's finest clay. Her eyelashes were long and dark with mascara. Her lips were glossed, the rest was natural. Her head leaned slightly my direction as she breathed softly. I was truly blessed. About a block before we got to the hotel, Tyson woke up crying. He hated being in the car seat. He had just started crawling about a week before. Leslie had told me about it one night, she was so proud of him. I was proud of him and at the same time sad because I wasn't there.

We finally got to the room as the sun began to fade behind the mountains. The light reflected off the rain that was always at the top of the ridge, revealing a heavenly view complete with a rainbow, and if you looked hard enough, there was a waterfall. We went in and up the elevator, playing make out as much as possible before the elevator stops. It was room 922, with a balcony and a beachside view. I opened the door as she gasped. The lighting was set low, with a hibiscus lying on the counter, her favorite flower; a note on her pillow saying, "Look under the bed." A candle sat outside on the balcony, blown out by the constant cool flowing air, but nonetheless it was there. She passed Tyson off to me as she bent down to look under the bed.

She came up with a box and said, "You are perfect. What's this for?"

I smiled and replied, "We weren't able to be together on our one-month anniversary."

One month sounds fast for how far we'd come, but the question to ask was not anything set in a book or on a stat sheet somewhere. Is there a timeline for love? Some may say yes; but me, I say it must have taken you a lifetime to figure that timeline out. She unwrapped it slowly and squealed when she saw what was inside: a complete set of Clinique Happy—the lotion, the lather, and the body wash.

She smiled then said before kissing me, "I ran out about a week ago. I love you, Adam Green."

"And I love you, Leslie Ranor. What do you want to do tonight?"

She laughed and said, "I want to sleep. I have to catch up from the jet lag. Right now, though, I'm kind of hungry. What is there to eat around here?"

"Anything under the sun, except for good Mexican food."

I sat on the bed and set Tyson down as she jumped on top of me, kissed me, and asked, "How much do you love me?"

I kissed her back and said staring into her eyes, "To the end of the earth, as long as the moon floats in the sky, as long as the rain falls, I will love you."

She smiled and said, "I can go without eating."

I laughed and said, "Well, I could if I'd eaten in the last thirty-six hours. Come on, sweetie, let's go downstairs and get some food; we'll catch up where we left off."

With a look of disappointment yet still happiness, she said okay.

Earlier that day, my roommate Travis had tried to give me a box of condoms.

I looked at him and asked, "What do condoms promote?"

"Sex."

"Exactly, and if I don't have any, I have an excuse for not doing it. I am going to try my best to hold out, and condoms don't help with that. Thanks anyway."

He looked at me like I was stupid. I wanted sex, but that's not what I was about. I wanted her.

We had pancakes for dinner. Afterwards we sat out front, watching all the tourists stroll by and held each other tightly, absorbing in the romantic night air. When we got back up to the room, we got ready for bed. While she got ready, I played with Tyson on the bed. He would crawl to me then smile, and I would push him over. With a look of determination, he would charge my new position then smile again. I picked him up and flew him around the room like Peter Pan. She made him a bottle to put him to sleep, and it did just that. We laid him on the floor, on top of a sheepskin blanket. He was exhausted and fell asleep very quickly. Now it was time for us to go to bed. I lay down first then she lay down next to me, slowly but surely pressing her backside against my pelvis. I lightly lifted her hair from the back of her neck and began to slowly peck at it. She moaned as she rolled her head over and grabbed mine, pulling my face to hers. She licked my nose and giggled, then kissed me as I kissed back. We slowly moved our tongues around in each other's mouths. I reached over her body and rolled her facing me.

I kissed her and said in a soft, seductive voice, "I love you."

I picked her chin up and ran my lips lightly up and down her neck down to her chest. Slowly, she took her shirt off and then began working on mine. I reached down while maintaining lip contact and gently slid her cheer shorts off. In unison, we went for mine as I let her take over. And there we were naked, our bodies gliding against each other as our lips were inseparable. She reached for my hand and slowly led it to her breast. After she was satisfied with my ability to arouse her senses, she lowered her hand, mapping out my body, slowly moving down. The warmth of her hand sent a stimulating chill down my back. I moved my hand down. She gasped and held me tight, digging her fingernails into me, sending a sensational feeling down both our spines. I continued to slowly rub her, our breaths heavy and in full heat now. We breathed deeply, allowing only the air from each other to pierce our lungs. She tightened her legs and began to twitch as she pulled me on top of her. I pulled her head into my chest as she ran her tongue lightly across it.

Then in a sensual voice, she asked, "Did you bring any condoms?"

I had to smile as I kissed her and said, "No, you know why?"

Her voice was heaving just as mine was as she asked, "Why?"

"Because I knew you would ask? I told you I was going to try my best to not sleep with you tonight? You have no idea how badly I want this, but I don't want to ruin anything; and whether or not you think it will, I need to not do this for myself. I want to show you that that's not what I'm about. You understand, don't you?"

She replied in a disappointed but still aroused voice, "Yes, I love you so much."

"I love you too."

I rolled off of her, kissed her once more, and held her tightly as she fell asleep. I had to wake up that morning to go run with my section; I had tried to get off but ended up having to go in just to run. As we lay there, I smiled, smelled her hair, and went to sleep.

I woke up at 0400 that morning, completely exhausted, to drive twenty miles back to base. I got dressed as quietly as possible, walked around to her side of the bed. I watched that angel sleep for a minute before kissing her forehead.

I whispered, "You are beautiful, and I love you," then bent down and did the same for Tyson.

On my way out the door, she moaned a groggy "I love you too, sweetie."

❧

When I got back to base, my roommates were trying to bug me for details, and I just told them, "I love her, and no, we did not do it."

They made fun of me as I just smiled, unable to get her out of my mind.

❧

I got back to the hotel around 10:00 and called her as I parked in the parking garage.

She said, "We're down at the beach."

I walked the block to the beach looking around for her. She was waving at me while sitting down on a bench feeding Tyson. She was wearing a black-and-white flowered bikini top and black shorts.

When I got to her, I bent down and gave her a kiss and asked, "How'd you sleep last night, beautiful?"

She smiled and enthusiastically said, "Amazing! How was your little run?"

I smiled and said, "Well, I was running, and three miles to me isn't that little. You're lucky I took a shower before I came back, because I didn't exactly smell like roses."

The blue-green ocean water and the palm trees painted a subtle scene in the background. The sand was smooth and white, and the ocean breeze blew freshly against us. We decided to go swim and challenge the ocean waves. I held Tyson above my head ducking down long enough for the next wave to get him excited. He would squeal and giggle as he saw the waves come at him. Right before they would get to him, I would pop him up just high enough to avoid the swells.

She would dance circles around me, then laugh and tell me, "Do you know how happy I am?"

I would just smile, because my happy place was there with her. There were no words to describe how I felt, so I didn't even try. She floated up to me as I held Tyson with my arms fully extended above my head, grabbed me, and squeezed, throwing one of her legs back.

She buried her head in my chest and said right before kissing me, "I never want this to end."

I kissed her back trying to stay balanced and not drop Tyson as the people around stared and gawked. We were in love, and we didn't care.

"Let um look," I'd say, and she'd say, "You're right, I don't care what they think."

It was amazing how we'd bridged a gap of space and time; a million miles apart, our struggles and triumphs both equally great. Different battlefields we fought, and now here we were, in paradise, falling more and more in love.

As the day began to fade, we walked along the beachfront on our way back to the hotel. I pushed Tyson in his stroller; he'd been officially worn out for the day as he slept soundly with the ocean waves crashing in the background as the gulls cawed overhead. Like an orchestra, the waves and breeze were the bass and the birds were the treble. We walked by a pavilion next to the local beach police station as a jazz band began to perform a street sideshow. I stopped and turned, and without a word grabbed her hand and pulled her in close. I delicately placed both my hands on her lower back as she placed hers on my shoulders and we began to dance. I'm sure we weren't dancing to good; we had the sand to compete with our steps and balance. Nevertheless, it was a romantic evening and one more seed that had been planted in our hearts.

Later that evening after the sun had set; I had a nice dinner set up at a Japanese steak house. I wanted this evening to be perfect. We sat out in the parking lot; we had a thirty-minute wait for a table. I looked over at Leslie, leaned in, and met her with a kiss. I reached in the center console and pulled out a ring box.

I stared into her eyes as she stared at the box, and as I opened it, I said, "Leslie, this is a promise ring. I love you so much. This ring is a promise of my love, a promise to hold you in my heart always."

She smiled and said, "It's beautiful, and Adam Green, I love you too. God, I love you. I promise to hold you in my heart and love you."

She was so beautiful as I slowly slid the ring onto her finger then pulled her hand up and kissed the ring.

I placed my hand in hers and said, "You are truly beautiful, and it's a miracle you're with me. I thank God every day."

She laughed and said, "You're a dork. I thank God, too, and I love you."

The dinner was excellent, and afterwards we walked on the strip by the beach. The moon was out and the stars were glistening. Feet in the sand, walking hand in hand beneath the palm trees, I twisted her around to face me and held both her hands.

She looked up at me and said, "You are perfect!" then kissed my neck. We rocked back and forth looking intently into each other's eyes as the cool evening breeze blew. The stars reflected off her eyes revealing a picture into her soul. The night was young, and our hearts through trials and tribulations seemed ancient. Life was good, you could almost say perfect. Now this moment, oh, what a magical moment, a moment that would be forever embedded in our hearts; a moment that, like all good moments, would end too soon.

We got back to the hotel. It was about 11:00 now, and we were both exhausted. The entire day had been so perfect, neither one of us wanted it to end. And as the clock started creeping toward midnight, we lay under the covers. She faced me and I her as we gazed into each other's eyes, looking directly into each other, when we simultaneously said, "I love you." We smiled and laughed, then she leaned in and kissed me. Passionate sparks started flying, and the love of a lifetime apart, and meant to be, began to quickly blossom. We began kissing each other's bodies and whispering sweet nothings. The lights were out, but the moon provided a perfectly illuminating mood. I softly ran my hand down the side of her body, caressing back and forth. She moaned and said seductively, "Oh, Adam. Oh, Adam. I love you so much."

Breathing hot and heavy but still maintaining my willpower to hold out, I said, "Leslie, I want you to be completely honest with me. Do you love me?"

She closed her eyes as she pulled me on top of her then kissed my chest and said, "Absolutely, I love you with all my heart."

I gently kissed her eyelids then asked, "Do you think it will ruin what we have if we have sex? Because I don't want to ruin anything."

She pulled my head down to hers and whispered in my ear "No, I love you too much. I always will."

Then before I could allow myself to become completely lost in the physical aspect of love, I asked again "Promise me, Leslie, promise me."

I pushed myself up above her as she said, "I promise you, Adam, you are my all." I kissed her again, and slowly, ever so gently, we became one—one life, one heart beating, one love. Just as day cannot exist without night, just as a ship cannot sail by itself, we existed through each other; a love strong enough to bring on the rain, strong enough to calm the seas. She was mine, and

I was hers, and for those magical moments in which the love of two young hearts became one, I knew we were special. The passions of love are not expressed through physical actions, they are expressed through what can only be called God's gift—love in its truest form.

The next few days went by fast, way too fast, and all the good times became just memories. We physically expressed our love every chance we got. And then she was gone. We would have to build upon the stones we had laid. In just a short amount of time, where other couples had just begun building their love in several months, we had done it in a time way too fast to comprehend, and yet the speed of it did not lessen the reality of it at all.

I kissed her right before she stepped off to board her plane then bent down and kissed Tyson and said, "I love your momma, yea, of course, you too."

He smiled and rubbed his little hand across his baby blue eyes. Then Leslie said, "I had a great time. Thank you for everything, I love you."

I kissed her again and said, "I love you too. You gotta go now before you miss your flight."

Just like a fire, we had burned strong, but now she was gone. As I watched her plane leave, I prayed a prayer of thanks. I kissed her picture and jokingly swore that I would not take a shower again because I didn't want to lose her smell, I didn't want to lose her touch that still lingered on my skin. I had snuck one of my shirts into her luggage before she left and wondered if she would find it. The sun was high and the air was hot and would have been miserable if I wasn't totally in love. I was, though, and hell itself couldn't make me feel any less than happy.

ROTTEN APPLES

LESLIE WAS TOUGH, a strong-willed, independent woman. These amazing and rare-to-find-together traits, however, were also her downfall. They were also our downfall. And just as fast as she had fallen in love with me, she fell back out. Five days—five days after she left—we broke up. My heart held on, though; it still does.

"I love you, Leslie. Goodnight," I said right before we got off the phone.

"Goodnight." She replied. I had heard "I love you" in return whenever I said it for a while now. When she didn't say it back to me, I questioned her about it.

"Don't I get an 'I love you too'?"

Then like a sack of bricks, she hit me with, "I've been thinking about that a lot lately, and I just don't know if how I feel about you is really love." My life so high on a pedestal was suddenly gone, and my heart hit the floor like an anvil.

Sounding shocked, I replied, "Are you going to break up with me?"

In a tone not her own, she replied, "No, I just don't know how I feel about us right now."

My heart kicked back in a little, and I replied in a less-than-happy tone, "Leslie, I love you and I know it's real, and I know everything you said, everything you did, was real too. If you need space I can give it to you. If you need time I'll give you that too. But I can't...do not ask me to try and reverse my feelings. I'll put them on pause—whatever you need, I'll do—but I cannot and will not take back any *true* words I have said."

She got angry and defensive then replied, "I'm not asking you to, I just don't know how I feel."

I quickly snapped back, "Well, I do. I do know how you feel. You know what, it's late there. I'm gonna let you get some sleep. Goodnight." I waited for a second for any kind of response, and when there was none, I hung up.

I called back the next day and apologized. The mood was still tense, and both of us tried to avoid talking about how she felt. We made hollow conversation. Just like everyone, has to watch a traffic accident as they drive by. I couldn't avoid bringing it up again. Her mood had gotten worse about it. She was confused, and I knew I should probably just drop the subject. Just as anyone in their right mind could not drop a baby, I couldn't drop the subject. I sighed holding back the waterfall of tears from spilling out my eyes and said, "Leslie, I love you, and I want you to be happy. But more than what I want, more than what you want, I want what God wants. Will you do me a favor, actually two favors? Will you, one, pray—pray long and hard about us? And two, for me, will you think about what love is to you? What does it mean to you? I will do the same. Will you do that for me?"

It hurt me so bad to know, and I did know that the best thing that had ever happened to me would slip away soon. She replied emotionally, but not crying, "Yes." We changed the subject for a second before I couldn't handle it any more.

In order to keep from beating a dead horse, I said goodnight then got off.

I prayed all night, unable to sleep. I asked God, "Please, God, I know what I want and what you want may be completely different things. You know my heart, God. I want her, I love her. But above what I want, I want what you want." Then a voice in the darkness replied to me, a voice I hadn't heard since I was a child. A voice I had ignored for years.

It said, "My son, she will come back to you, just give her time. I love you, my son, and have only the best intentions for you. I am the alpha and the omega, the beginning and the end. I am the air you breathe, the day and the night. Have faith, and she will return." I cried knowing what this meant. I walked out on my balcony and sat down in my old beat-up blue chair. The breeze blew softly against my face as I buried it in my hands and let the floodgates of my eyes open up. Then I thought of what love is to me.

When we finally talked the next day, it was quick and straight to the point. I said, unable to sound like myself, "So what do you think? What do you think about us?" Then I said, "Wait, I have something to say before you talk." I paused and continued, "Know that if we break up, I will not be able to be your friend. I cannot go through that again. I spent almost four years being that, and it broke my heart every day. If you break up with me, you may want to make this conversation the longest one you ever had with me, because once it's done, you won't hear from me again...I promised you, Leslie, I will always be there for you, and I will keep that, even if we break up. But I will not go out of my way, you will have to come to me."

She said sadly, "I want this to be mutual, and I want to still be friends."

I snapped back, "Leslie, know this. Know that this is not mutual in anyway. Know that I do not want this by any means, and know that I can't be just friends."

Then she said, "Well, then I guess we're through then. Why can't this be mutual?"

There it was, my heart had been ripped in half. As I fought back the tears, I said, "Because I love you too much, and always will. Mutual is when two people feel the same way, and I thought we did. I was wrong. Why are you doing this? Can I ask why? What did I do wrong?"

She said with clear confusion in her voice, "I'm just not ready for a relationship."

I wanted to say something smart back but held my tongue and replied calmly, "If you got anything to talk about, let's talk; otherwise, I got to go."

I tried to bury my feelings, but it seemed like the farther I pushed them down, the more it hurt. I got a fifth of rum and an energy drink. If I couldn't bury my feelings, maybe I could drown them. Shot after shot I got drunk, and more drunk. I never relapsed to alcohol to take care of pain and shouldn't have made that exception. I leaned over the toilet, praying to the porcelain god, and painfully vomited. I screamed in my bathroom, "I love you, why?" then kept vomiting until I passed out on the bathroom floor using a shoe and a sock as a pillow and a washcloth as a blanket. My buddy Mike walked in and picked me up while I was still unconscious and carried me to his bed, after taking a picture, of course. My rack was a top bunk which he slept on for the night.

He said to our other roommate Travis, "He and Leslie must have broken up. I've gotten drunk with him a million times and never seen him this bad."

The next few months were the roughest of my life. It's weird how you can feel better in Iraq getting shot at or blown up than you can trying to heal a broken heart. We kept talking occasionally for a little while; short, simple, hollow conversations. Every time I heard her voice, it tore my heart again, and still I couldn't let go. Then I heard from a reliable source that she had been sleeping around. I never believed it. My buddies told me, as well as the whole town back home. They would say, "Dude, she used you for a trip to Hawaii."

But I knew and I told them, "I know she didn't use me, and this is how I know. She initiated everything.

With the exception of 'I love you,' she said it first or moved toward it first. Besides, she said 'I love you' after she agreed to come out to Hawaii."

Then they would ask, "Well, did you at least get some?"

To which I would sincerely reply, "That's mine and her business?"

Other buddies would say, "Dude, she did you wrong. Why do you still hold on?"

And I would say, "Because I pray, and I know what's gonna happen. I love her and will always."

The rumor I had heard, though, about her sleeping around, I had to know; I just had to. Both our phones were down so we kept up on e-mail. I had broken my phone over my knee in an emotional rage. Honestly, it was probably the best thing to give us some necessary space.

I finally got a new phone and knew she could use another to call me. To get in touch with her, I ended up e-mailing her.

> Hey Leslie, how are you doing? I'm doin' good. I really need to talk to you. Will you give me a call soon? Please.

I had to hear from her that she was seeing someone. I just had to know. I didn't want to know, but for me

I needed to know. The response to that was not what I was hoping for.

> Great!! And no I probably won't because, I DONT have a phone!! lol sorry!! It's still broke, and I can't get a new one till next month when we upgrade!! Or I may switch companies so I may get a new number!! I lost everyone's number in my old phone so needless to say I haven't been chatting with ANYONE!! Lol

Now I didn't take this how she had hoped I'd believe. I took it as "I have a new guy I'm talking to, so I don't want to be bothered by your memory." I knew she was lying, and that pissed me off, so I replied,

> Hey I hope your doin' good, but I'm really disappointed in you. You're better than that. Why would you lie to me? I know you've been sleeping with someone. It hurts me knowing you're gonna end up in the same situations you were in before. You are so stupid for doing this to yourself. Tyson needs a mom to be around, not a little teenage girl sleeping around. He's a great kid, why would you do that to him? Why would you lower yourself to that level? Leslie, I do not mean for this to be mean. I know it comes across that way. Honestly though, I have the best of intentions and hope that this will open your eyes. If who I heard you were sleeping with is true, I know him and guys like him, and you will end up getting your heart broken again, which in turn will break mine again. I really want to know why we broke up; you never

> gave me a real reason. You know the whole town says you used me for a trip to Hawaii, and they're all pissed at you. I don't believe that though. I know you better than that. If the next guy treats you worse than I do, well, I feel bad for you, because you only deserve the best. Be smart. Think of yourself, think of your son, be a mother. Please call me. I got my phone back. In case you forgot, my number is (807) 734-7492.

I probably shouldn't have been that harsh, but I was. I could have just said, "Well, will you borrow someone's phone? This is really important," but I didn't. She replied,

> Ooo yea, I got a new one too... 1-800-SCREW-YOU!!!
>
> You know good and well I am a great mom, you asshole. I can't believe you would say something like that. You really screwed up, Adam. I don't know why the hell you would send such hateful message!! Say what you want Adam!! But do not put my parenting down!! How foolish of you!! I am a single mother!! And I am trying to make it on my own. Don't you dare put me down!! There's nothing worse than someone kicking you while you're down!! Oo and I broke up with you because I just really didn't see myself with you in the future!! O.K.!! I didn't have that strong of feelings for you and no, I never used you! I know why you're writing all this nonsense and it's because you need closure!! But you keep egging everything on!! I am not with anyone!! Just to let you know!!

> I am doing what I told you I would do!! So you're sitting here telling me to grow up and that I don't know what it is to be a parent... How the hell would you possibly know how it feels to be a parent!! Especially a single parent!! Before you start talking shit, walk a mile in my shoes!! Ok and here's your closure you need!! It's over......forever!! Oo and no, you're not the best thing that ever happened to me.... Just to let you know, I'll find better!! Better than someone telling me I am horrible, and can't be a good mother!! You're so selfish and crude!! So keep doing your thing, getting drunk!! And don't forget to read your Bible, Proverbs 33:8 is a pretty good one!! ADIOS

Now when I said, "because you only deserve the best," I hadn't meant it the way she took it. I never used the Bible as a bribery tool, but nonetheless I would look it up. I replied,

> Leslie, I was told by someone you were sleeping with someone. This was by a very reliable source—a person I would trust with my life. And yes, I am after closure. I only question your ability to be a mother if what I am being told is true. I am not in any way trying to insult you ok. You just gave me so many different BS reasons for breaking up with me. I know while we were together I did nothing wrong, and I guess that's why it toys with me so bad. I would have rather done something wrong. I was told that you basically had a friend-with-benifits, ok, not that you were seeing someone. If that's

true, that is where I am insulting you. Get a boyfriend, get whatever you want, I know you can. You're beautiful, it won't be too hard. Oh, I know you didn't use me for a trip out here, you just broke up with me less than a week after you got back and that's why people think you did. I do not think that, though, I know better. If you are sleeping with someone, you're BETTER than that. And yes, Leslie, I hope and I still pray that you'll have better than me. I know all your past boyfriends and that's why I say that. If the next guy doesn't treat you good...Leslie you are a wonderful girl and only deserve the best. I'm not saying the thing about the town to bother you, just to bring it to your attention. I have prayed for you before us, I prayed for you while we were together, and I will continue to pray for you. This is my promise to you. I don't want sympathy, I don't want you back. What I do want, though, is for you to know that yes, you are a great mother, and no, I haven't been in your shoes. Have you been in mine though? I have moved on as have you, but I still care about you. I hate it, but I guess I always will. It's my curse. That is why I said the things I said, and it was very immature on both our parts to write hateful stuff like we did. I'm sorry if what I heard was a rumor, but if it's true, the words I wrote are true, because you are better than that. We need to both grow up, Leslie, and the mature thing for us to do would be to talk and resolve our problems. Not just for myself. You're over me, I'm over you, but us talking once, just a nice conversation, would be very mature and

> allow us to settle some stuff. You are an awesome mother and Tyson is an awesome kid, and yes, you are doing an exceptionally well job raising him. I'm done being a prick. Know this, though, Leslie, if the next guy doesn't treat you as good, or better than I did, he ain't the one either. Call me sometime, think about it. What's it gonna hurt to be mature? I'm not calling you immature, I know your situation, kind of, and as I said several times, you are handling it in the most mature manner. I love you, Leslie, not in the same way we used to. It's more of a brother-sister kind of love now. I know I said a million times if the next one doesn't treat you as good as I did, he ain't the one either. I say this because I don't want to see you get hurt, and I know you will end up hurting yourself. I hope you can see what I'm trying to say. Good luck with everything life throws at you, and I will pray for you still.
>
> Adam
>
> P.S. Hey, I'm done talkin' to you from hereon, it's on you, and trust me, you'll wise up someday, a month, a year, 10 years from now you'll look back. Proverbs doesn't have 33 books in it, only 31, so what verse was it you wanted me to read?

I really didn't expect to hear back from her. Considering the things I said, she probably shouldn't have. But surprisingly she did, and that, as slim as it may be, meant there was still hope, still a chance.

> Sorry, it was proverbs 8:33. I put it in wrong!! But I'm through with everything!! For real...I really just want to chill, I don't need to talk to you on the phone. The only person that can give you closure is yourself!! Because it's only you holding yourself back!! And if we talk you'll hold on to it!! So I'm going to say bye for now!!

She was somewhat right; if we would have talked, I would definitely have held on. But in order to move on, I needed to hear from her. I needed to hear her voice, simply because her voice was the only thing I could believe. The fact that I knew I would not hear her voice, despite the desire I had to hear it, gave me hope. It gave me hope because I knew if I didn't hear it, she would still hold on. I could still hold on.

Days became weeks, weeks became months that I didn't hear from her—months that I counted down to the second until I would see her again. Slowly and steadily I moved on, still holding on to her memory, but the pain had lessened. Evenings were the worst time of day for me. Sunsets spent alone, the cool air brushing my skin alone. When it rained, I died all over again; and when I walked around the wilderness on training operations, I saw her. Driving down the road, I saw her next to me. At festivals, seeing all the happy couples, all the kids running around, I saw all the things I could have had and once did have. Whenever I would walk by another woman, I saw her and I imagined the warmth that I once felt on my skin. It was tough. I no longer went to the beach; hell, I very rarely even left my room. I try to live life to the fullest, you know, look at the glass half full. I do not live with regrets, and never will. I didn't look at the past and ask, "What can I do to change it?" I looked simply at the future, and somehow, without a plan or goal in mind, thought what can I do to change it? I knew I had planted the seeds and knew beyond the shadow of a doubt that someday she would look back and see me. And when that day comes, we would finally be together again. My biggest question, though, was when would that day come?

I would see her two more times before I left for Iraq. Once at church, which broke me in two. She smiled and I waved, we said hi and bye. She had a boyfriend again, the stalker from work. He treated her like crap, and I knew she was miserable; I could hear it in her voice. She was no longer peppy, no longer laughed as much. Nonetheless she persisted, despite her misery. I knew why she dated him, she did it because she knew it would tick me off, and it did. The next time I saw her was my last night home. I'd been driving around aimlessly for the last few hours trying to find something to do, something to take my mind off of reality. It was dark now, and as my headlights hit the sign "Salado 7 miles," I knew what I had to do. I drove up her driveway, placed my truck in park, rolled up the window halfway. I took one last drag of my cigarette then put it out, smothering the cherry in the ash tray. I had started smoking again after she broke up with me. Quite frankly, I didn't care about my health or what anyone thought about my bad habit. Not even her, she didn't seem to care about me, so I didn't care what she thought. I stepped out and zipped up my leather jacket and buttoned my cuffs. I walked up to the door, stood there for a moment thinking about what to say, and when nothing came to mind, I decided it was time to knock. She came down the stairs and opened it, speechless. Both of us just stared for a moment, almost lost for words, until I broke the ice. "Leslie, you wanna go for a walk?" The weather was kind of cold, but it was still a nice night.

She smiled shyly as she wiped a strand of hair from her face then said, "Sure, let me grab my coat."

I took off my jacket and said, "Don't worry about it."

She took the jacket and we began to walk. In silence we walked, head forward, eyes forward, both to afraid to look at the other. Her arms were crossed and I had my hands in my pockets. "I leave tomorrow. I just thought you might want to know," I said, trying to sound sincere.

She stopped and faced me, I took a few more steps then did the same, and she said, "Thanks for telling me. I'll pray for you. But why did you come out here, Adam? I know it wasn't to let me know something I already knew."

I smiled and said, "You caught me." She laughed then I continued, "Leslie, I just wanted to see your face, I wanted to tell you… that the last few months have been the hardest of my life. I'm not asking to take you back, because I don't know if I can. I'm still hurting. I know you've moved on. I guess I came by just to see you before I left."

She replied, "Well, what do you think?"

I smiled, placed my hands on her elbows as her eyes slowly began to well up, and said, "You know what I think. I've always thought the same thing and always will." My touch must have brought back memories as her tears lightly fell. The moonlight reflected the tears as they fell to the ground in slow motion. The teardrops told me all I needed to know. Now the reason for my coming here was clear. I had come to find out whether or not she was still mine. And those tears said it all. She still was...

DO YOU BELIEVE IN MIRACLES?

I THOUGHT BACK while on patrol to the last thing I remembered saying to her, before I came back to the land that God forgot. "You've put me through hell; it was nice to see you again. Really, it was, but I don't know if I can feel the same way I used to. I made you a promise, Leslie. Do you remember what I said?"

With a tear in her eye, she said, "Yes..."

I cut her off before she could continue, saying in a hollow voice. "I will always be there for you, if you want. I'm not goin' out of my way anymore. I've done everything I could think of. I tried to be your friend, I gave you space and time, and now I'm going back to Iraq and there's nothing I can do. Leslie, I'm gonna miss you. I care about you, and it's my curse I always will." I looked deep into her eyes for the last time as I said good-bye. I turned slowly and walked away.

As I walked away, I heard her whimpering, "Good-bye, don't go, don't go." I never looked back as a tear slowly formed and rolled down my cheek. I didn't even blink or make an attempt to wipe it. This was the last conversation, the last time I saw her, my last memory of her—the memory I hated to hang on to, but like a vice I couldn't let go. I knew I would probably never get back with her. She once again had a boyfriend who again treated her like crap. She was confused, and I realized now that she would have to figure it out on her own. She was now on her time. My time was up; I'd done and said all I could think of.

I needed to focus; I needed to do my job. We were back in Iraq, my second time. I'd been here for going on two months now. I never kept times or dates; to me knowing just made the time drag on. I knew my birthday would be in a few weeks, but other than that I didn't know, and quite frankly I didn't care. I'd lost all the will to care over the past few months. I was a hollow man. I hated it, I hated myself. I hated her, but I still loved her.

We were in a much better part of Iraq than last time; however, it was still nowhere near good. There hadn't been any KIAs yet, but we still had a handful of wounded. Just the other day, while we were out on a routine patrol, we had an RPG shot at us. As it whizzed past us toward the back of the patrol, it hit a wall about ten meters behind our last man. The blast threw shrapnel through his hand, straight through like a paper hole punch.

Now, though, we were convoying to our re-supply point when we came under small arms fire, from AK47s and RPGs. We halted the convoy in order to gain fire superiority. Then when we finally came to a complete stop, they hit the third vehicle, the vehicle behind me, with an IED. It was a big one, and it looked like a direct hit, from my standpoint. I ran up with LCpl. Nelson, a guy in my team, as I yelled at him. "Nelson, look for secondaries then set up security! Try and find a place with some cover too!" Everything came second nature to us; we had drilled it a million times over into our heads. As I ran through the dust and still-falling debris, I saw through the passenger-side window. The humvee was intact still but had been caught on fire. The fire wasn't too big yet, but as soon as it hit the fuel lines, it would go up like a match. The passenger, VC, was already out of his gear and leaning over trying to get the unconscious driver's gear off. Cpl. Jeffers, the VC, ripped and tore at it with no avail then pulled out a knife and began to cut it off. I finally got over to the driver's side door, opened it, and yelled, "Jeffers, I got him, get out!" I could tell he couldn't hear me but understood what I was saying. I pulled LCpl. Fields, the driver, out and began to drag him in between the nearest safe-looking buildings. I got him there and placed my fingers on his radial, feeling for a pulse. It was weak but steady and still there, but he was still unconscious. I used a trick our corpsman had taught me on the last deployment.

He used to say in his deep southern accent, "You could wake a man up from anything short of a coma by pinching the back of the arm high on the tricep."

Sure enough, as soon as I pinched, his eyes began to flutter; and in a groggy, pissed off voice, he said, "What the hell, man?"

I laughed at him and said, pointing, "You just got hit, yea, you were in that burning humvee right there." I checked a few more vitals to make sure he'd be all right. I checked his pulse once more; it was getting better, his eyes were beginning to un-dilate, and the few cuts he had had started to scab up; he'd be fine. I told him, "Stay right here man till I get back. You got plenty of cover, just stay alert."

Before I ran off, he grabbed me and said, "Hey, thanks, corporal."

I looked at him and said, "It's not your day today kid, it's not your day. Just keep cover and shoot back." I ran back to the blast sight to start helping out again as I thought back to a week earlier.

I had gotten a letter from Leslie, the first and only she'd ever written me. I remembered I hesitated to open it; I contemplated throwing it away or just saving it till the end of the deployment. Finally, after battling with myself over how much I hated her and how much I didn't want to ever hear another thing about her, much less from her, I thought about how much I loved her and decided to open it. As I opened it, I smelled her scent, I felt her presence; and as I began to read, I heard her voice taking over the words. And suddenly she was there in the middle of the battlefield with me reading it to me again.

Dear Adam,

I know this is the first letter of mine you've gotten; for that I'm sorry. You always told me if I had something to say that I really wanted to say, to just say it. I have to get this off my conscience. Well, there's just so much I want to say and somehow the words escape me, I just don't know how to say it. Nothing seems like it would be sufficient. I know you probably don't even want to hear from me. I think there are some things, though, that are worth being said.

I'm not the best at saying what I'm about to say, but I want you to know this is how I really feel. What you said to me when we broke up, well, pretty much everything came true, you were right. I'm sorry I was blind, I'm sorry I didn't listen. I guess what I'm trying to say is I love you and I always have. I just needed some time to realize it.

I was cleaning out my closet the day you left when I came across my little collection box. I opened it, and all the stuff I had in there reminded me of you. I picked up the shirt you snuck into my luggage before I left and smelled it. That smell, oh that smell, it brought back so many good times. Times I had only had with you. And suddenly it was like I could feel your arms around me, holding me tight and secure by your touch. That's when I called Tanner and told him I'm done, I'm through. I told him I loved someone else, I told him I had all along. That person was you. I never gave you a real reason for breaking up with you, and I know I should have. Not having one probably drove you crazy. I guess I didn't give you one because I honestly didn't have one. I was just confused. You were right to walk away when you left, I should have told you right there how I felt. It hurt me so bad, seeing you leave. You never looked back. I couldn't contain the tears. You have always been so nice to me and to Tyson. Before and after we broke up, you made a promise to me; you said you would always be there for me if I wanted you to. Well I do, I want you to be there for me, and I want to be there for you.

"And maybe you're gonna be the one that saves me, and after all you're my wonder wall," a line from my favorite song. Adam Green, you're my wonder wall, will you be the one that saves me? Do you remember the night we danced on the beach? Or earlier that night when you gave me the promise ring? You said, "This ring is a promise of my love, a promise that I will always hold you in my heart." Adam, that was a two-way promise. I know you believe everything happens for a reason, and that there's no need in living a life full of regrets. But if there was one thing I could change, one thing I'd have done different, one thing I regret, I'd still be with you and you'd still be loving me. There's so much more I want to say, so many more feelings I feel. Please, Adam, be mine again, I love

> you so much. I pray for your safety every day. Come home to me, Adam. Come home to me, I love you.
>
> Love,
> Leslie

Just like that I was hooked again, I wanted to write her back, but at the same time, I was still bitter. I wanted her to know my pain.

I carried the letter around in my flak jacket everywhere I went. I had it strategically placed on the left side, guarding my heart. It made me feel sometimes like her heart was there beating in sync so close to mine. It made me feel safe and impenetrable. Now, though, it was back to reality.

The bullets started flying again as I ran back toward the humvee, like a bat out of hell. I ran around the backside to take cover. Jeffers was on the other end. He looked back to see me and said, "Good to have some company, I got eyes on." It was good to know where they were, but the vehicle would be engulfed in flames in a minute or two if we were lucky.

I yelled, "Where's your gunner?"

As we shot back, he said, "He got thrown, he's in the IED crater." I looked at him as if to say, "Well then, why the hell are you still here?"

Common sense kicked in as I yelled, "Jeffers, listen up. We don't have much time before this vehicle goes up in flames. I'm gonna run over to get him. You lay down a wall of lead for me. As soon as I get there, you get away from the humvee. I will pop smoke before I come out. Then you give me another barrage of bullets to cover me." He looked at me like I'd lost my mind. Truth be told, I kind of had

Then he said, "Okay, got it."

I smiled and said, "On three! One! Two! Three!" I ran faster than I'd ever ran before, weaving back and forth trying to be bulletproof, or at least dodge them. About ten more steps and I'd be to the crater. The bullets whistled by me, or were hitting the ground all around. I felt a little sting in my left leg. Almost there, it was probably just my leg cramping up. That's what it felt like. Finally I was there; I slid face first into the hole, low crawling once I got in. I saw the gunner LCpl. Ellis lying there on the opposite side bloody and broken. He was conscious, calm, and in his own little world. He was reclining on the wall of the crater sipping some water out of a canteen.

He looked lost, as he said in an oddly happy voice. "Hey, Cpl. Green. You gonna help me out? I don't think I'm gonna make it, but that's okay."

He took another sip as I rushed toward him and said, "I'm gonna get you out. Today ain't your day buddy. I'm gonna need your help, okay?"

"Yea, hey, corporal. I think you're bleeding." I looked at him with a serious face as I pulled the tourniquet off my flak.

"Okay, Ellis, your arm's broken. This is gonna hurt, but I need you to be strong. Just close your eyes and think you're back home, or about Jennifer, your fiancée." His arm was more than broken; just above the elbow down was completely gone. He was bleeding out fast.

He didn't know his arm was that bad off, and I wanted it to stay that way. I had to use all the willpower and bearing I had to not vomit or make a disgusted face. I cinched the tourniquet down tight and the bleeding slowly receded but didn't fully cut off. He probably had about ten minutes of life in him. I said as I popped smoke. "You ready to go, buddy? I'm gonna get you out of here, just stay with me."

He looked at me, his face getting paler and paler, and said, "Corporal, your leg's bleeding pretty bad."

I smiled and said, about the same time the humvee went up in flames, "Yea, I'm ready to get out of here too, man." I hoisted him up on my shoulders and crawled out of the crater. Jeffers had already started providing covering fire as I trudged through the smoke. About twenty meters more and we'd be safe. That's when I heard the whiz of the RPG fly by. The explosion knocked me down; Jeffer's body smashed my head into the concrete as he rolled off of me. Thank God for a helmet.

I heard someone yell "Grenade!" then I saw it rolling toward us through the smoke. It was too far away to kick back and too close to avoid shrapnel. I threw my body over LCpl. Ellis, using my body as a shield. *Boom.* I got up, grabbed him by the back of his flak jacket, then drag him in between the buildings into the safest alley I could find.

Then I yelled, "Corpsman up!" I stood up and leaned against the wall to catch my breath and took a sip of water. I wiped the sweat and grime off my face, leaving a bloody smear. The corpsman ran around the corner. I yelled above the chaos, "Hey, doc, get him; his arm's all kind of messed up and he'll be gone soon if we don't get him outta here fast." I got back down and began to help doc patch him up. The firefight stopped almost in unison with when we got him stabilized and ready to be medevac'd out.

Then doc looked up at me and said, "Thanks, man. He'd have died without that tourniquet you put on. Hey, are you okay? You're lookin' kind of flushed." I was wobbling back and forth as the colors started to mesh together like a tie-dye shirt. Apparently, the backside of my trousers was peppered with shrapnel. I must have been shot, too; yes, yes I was, that's what the pain in my leg was. That's where the blood was from.

I placed my hand on the wall behind me to steady myself. Losing my balance quickly, I responded, "Yea, doc, I'm fi..." I lost consciousness. Black, nothing, and then...

There she was, magnificent in her splendor, fields of green waving in the background, a beautiful white dove soared overhead. The sun was bright as it was on its descent, but for some reason I didn't even feel the need to squint. A lake lie beyond the pasture, crystal blue. She was there holding out her hand as if she were awaiting a dance. The light perfectly reflected off her skin, letting on no shadows. She was wearing a white silk robe draped modestly over one shoulder. Her hair blew freely in the soft cool breeze, and she said with a smile in the most angelic voice, "Come home to me, Adam, come home." I reached up and grasped her hand, speechless. Her hand was smooth as velvet and softer than silk. I was at peace, I was secure in her touch. She smelled of fresh coffee and a perfume I couldn't quite name. Her eyes glowed resembling the lake behind her. Barefoot, she stood tall. Golden jewelry on her wrist and her ears. Her lips shined ruby red, moist with gloss. Then together, we swayed back and forth, dancing, holding each other tightly as I felt the heavenly warmth of her body pressed against mine.

I smiled lightly as I breathed gently on her neck and said, "I'm comin' home, Leslie. I'll be home. I love you," as an invisible force took us slowly into the sunset.

Leslie was back home feeding Tyson. For some reason, he wasn't himself today. He was whining and fussy, more noticeably than usual. She had done a few chores around the house; she vacuumed and dusted off the cabinets. She looked through her photo album as she fed Tyson. Pictures of Adam jogged her memory and she smiled. She looked at Tyson and said, "What do you think about Leslie Amber Green? I like it." She smiled and with bliss said, "Leslie Amber Green." She got Tyson to sleep for a minute; finally she had some time to relax. She sat down on the couch, crossed her legs and arms, lay on her back, then let out a sigh. She reached over and grabbed his picture, smiled and kissed it, then said, "I love you, Adam Green." Then something came over her, something odd. She was completely and utterly happy. She felt like dancing. She stood up slowly and seductively held out her hand as if awaiting a partner. In a soft tone, a voice surpassing the word "angelic," she said, "Come home to me, Adam, come home." And then the extraordinary happened. She felt his touch; she could really feel his hand in hers. She felt his breath gently on the side of her neck. She smelled his skin and slowly wrapped her arms across her chest, ducked her head, and began to dance, swaying side to side. She let the silent music of the ceiling fan and gentle breeze flowing through the open windows take her away, then smiled and quietly whispered, "I love you, Adam; you're my wonder wall."

Ring, ring, ring. Upset now, the phone had ruined the mood. She picked it up; it was her mom. "Hey, Leslie, would you get the mail please?" She took her time walking out the door. When she got outside, she began to skip down the sidewalk to the mailbox. She hadn't skipped since she was a child, but she didn't care. She didn't have a worry in the world. She was absolutely and truly in love, and that's all she was sure of, that's all she cared about. She opened the mailbox and there on the top was a letter from him. It was sandy and dirty, crumpled and reeked of sweat. Over the seal, there was a drop of blood, and she smiled. She walked over to the bench outside the front door and sat down. She looked out beneath the shade of the mighty oak that leaned over her. The old wooden picket fence stood sturdy. The grass was exactly the right height. There were no weeds in the yard. The garden to her left housed three healthy rose bushes, two red rose bushes on the outside, and a white bush in the middle. She smiled gently as she brushed the hair away from her face, tucking it behind her ear, then began to sort the bills from the rest. She looked up at the sunset through the tall oak trees as the breeze almost too suddenly stopped. She thought for a minute of him until...

Ring, ring, ring. It was Adam's mom; she was surprised. She hadn't really talked with her since she and Adam broke up. She picked up the phone and in a happy, energetic voice said, "Hello, Mrs. Green!" Mrs. Green was crying softly on the other end, which threw her off guard. Her smile and energy quickly changed as she said, "Mrs. Green, please no, don't tell me, please no."

She looked around for anything to hold on to, left, right, then back again. When she looked back to the left, three rose petals fell stealthily to the ground. The first red petal hit softly and now lay dormant as a white petal came to rest just slightly on the edge of the first petal, and now the third working its way to the ground through a spiraling maze of air finally decided to settle right on top of the white. The reds sandwiched the white leaving just a sliver showing. She looked up to the sky holding back the tears then glanced back to the petals on the ground. It was clear now; it was a broken heart. It was her broken heart. Unable to contain the tears, she let herself go.

Mrs. Green, still sobbing, said, "Adam died today, about thirty minutes ago…he was in a hospital in Germany for two days. I don't know what happened, but they told me he lost too much blood due to the nature of his wounds. The funeral will be Tuesday at 3:00, visitation Monday at 7:00." Leslie was crying heavily now, holding his letter as tight as she could muster against her heart.

She said, trying to sound strong, but her voice saying completely different, "Okay, thank you for telling me. Are you okay, Mrs. Green?"

Mrs. Green slowly replied, "He loved you Leslie, he always had. He talked and asked about you every time we heard from him. They said right before he died, he said, 'I'm coming home, Leslie. I'll be home. I love you.' I have to go now. Good-bye."

She walked back inside, legs feeling weak, then collapsed on the couch. The news hit her hard. She smelled the letter which still smelled of sweat. Then kissed it before opening it. The tears continued welling and began to steadily drip on the envelope. She opened it and paused for a moment, just reflecting before she read it. She wiped her eyes, clearing away the mascara, and quietly began to read.

Leslie,

Your favorite quote "To err is human, to forgive divine" (Alexander Pope). I didn't want to be right; I wanted you to be happy and successful. And I know by me being right you were neither. I know you needed time, and it truly broke my heart giving it to you. I had so many different thoughts and emotions running through my mind every day since we've been apart. I tried countless times to get you off my mind, but could not. I can't count on one hand how many times a day something made me think of you. I questioned myself a million times over. What did I do wrong? Where did we go wrong? Is this just a bad dream? You were not there. It hurt. Leslie, it truly rebroke my heart every morning I woke up. You were in my heart every day and still are. After my heart broke, every morning when I woke up, it broke again knowing that you were gonna hurt yourself and there was nothing I could do to stop it. I never stopped loving you, I never will. I never will!

You are an amazing woman and Tyson is an amazing kid. Just so you know, I cried when I left, when I walked away, because just as I made a promise to you, that I will always keep. I made another promise to my marines. I said to them, "I love you, guys, and every single one of ya'll will come back before I do. I got nothing to live for, yea I got a family, but most of ya'll have wives or girlfriends. I am obsolete in this light. You WILL come home to them if I have anything to do about it." Leslie, I will be there for you, and I want you to be there for me. I love you and always will. These two promises, however, do not contradict. I've always been there for you, and I always will. I guess what I'm trying to say is, I'm not going out of my way on this tour to survive. I'm going out of my way to make sure the man to my left and the man to my right survive. I always said everything happens for a reason, and I truly believe that. Leslie, everything you need is just an inch below the surface. Everything you need is in your heart. Leslie, I am in your heart and always will be. I will come home to you. You are my home, Leslie. I live and breathe you. If I don't make it back, know that I love you and will have a home waiting for you in heaven. I love you, Leslie, always remember you are loved. Raise Tyson to be a good man, and teach him how to treat a woman.

I will be home in September and would love to see you and Tyson. Please write me back this time. We are both on the same page; we both feel the same way. God made struggles that we might triumph. I love you, Leslie Amber Ranor, I love you so much.

Love,
Adam

Amazing grace how sweet the sound, that saved a wretch like me. I once was lost but now I'm found, was blind but now I see.

Leslie rolled up her window as the rain began to pour after the funeral. Her black gold-studded purse with an envelope sat in the passenger seat. She placed her head on the steering wheel and began to cry. Finally, she gained her composure enough to drive, wiping away the tears. She began to drive back to her house, still fighting the tears; and as fate would have it, her rear passenger tire went flat. The tears began to roll again, then her cries slowly turned to laughter. She reached over and grabbed the envelope then stepped out into the rain in her black blouse and knee-high skirt. She spread her arms wide and spun around dancing with the rain. The letter, addressed "Adam," rested in her right hand. Then the majestic sky opened up, still raining on her, but the light put her in what looked to be a stairway to heaven. She smiled and danced and said, "I love you, Adam Green. I wrote you back." She laughed with heavenly bliss then said, "I didn't want to leave it at your grave. I wanted to hand it to you personally. I never thought I'd get the chance to, but since you're here right now, I'll just give it to you." She held out her hand like the statue of liberty now as a lone dove swooped down and grabbed it. The dove rose higher and higher, the letter secured by its talons. Not fazed, her eyes followed the letter until she could no longer see it, then said, "I have it memorized; it's simple." And she began to quote her letter to the heavens.

Dear Adam,

I love you, I love you, I love you!